Richmond Booe, Wanted in Texas

By

Lazarus Barnhill

Deep Indigo Books
Published by Indigo Sea Press
Winston-Salem

Deep Indigo Books
Indigo Sea Press
PO Box 26701
Winston-Salem, NC 27114

For information regarding bulk purchases of this book, digital purchase and special discounts, please contact the publisher at indigoseapress@gmail.com

Cover design by Pan Morelli
Manufactured in the United States of America
ISBN 978-1630664794

To Debbie J, Brian B, the Booe and Bartholomew families.
Thank you for your goodness.

Chapter 1

Fire in the Barn

When he was certain the barn concealed him from being seen by anyone in the house, he emerged from the tree line. Making sure the horse's steps stayed within the copious tracks of cattle and horses, he gazed in every direction and listened for any sound of human activity.

"You got to love a barn with a back door, Jack," he muttered to the sorrel pony. "It's a miracle and just when we need one."

Dismounting as quietly as possible, he turned the wooden peg and opened the small back door slowly. For half a minute he listened and waited as his eyes grew accustomed to the dark interior, then he led his mount inside.

The soft dirt within muffled the sound of their steps. Quickly he determined the barn was large enough to have four or six large stalls in the back part as well as a small open corral. A young, well-formed paint raised its head above the top rail of one of the pens, watching the silent man lead his horse into the barn.

"Here you go, Jack. Meet your new neighbor."

He opened the gate to the farthest pen, against the barn wall, and led the sorrel inside. For a moment he stood wrestling with the decision of whether or not to pull the saddle off of his horse before finally unbuckling it and sliding it to the ground. Off came the saddle blanket and he pulled the reins off as well.

"If somebody does come in here looking and sees you with a saddle on, Jack, there won't be any question that you don't belong. Next them boys be looking for me."

He opened the side of his saddle bags that wasn't loaded

1

down with bags of money and pulled out three more revolvers, sticking them in his belt. Those, along with the two Peacemakers he wore, were all he could manage to carry and use at if it came to a gunfight. He left the two-shot derringer and the big Colt Dragoon packed away. Chances were, if it came down to it, he would never have time to reload a cap-and-ball pistol anyway. As he dragged his gear and the saddle to the back corner of the stall, pulled off his duster and hat and dropped them on top and covered the little pile with hay, he tried to guess what he might be facing if the posse tracked him to the barn.

"Just got to hope they went the other way down the fork in the creek, Jack," he whispered. "A dozen of them is a lot to fight. And it's got to be a fight right here, cause you're too tired to run anymore and them boys are too fresh." He stood before the pony, rubbing his long nose. "If it comes to it, Jack, I'll bust out and face them. I won't let them burn you here in the barn."

What was his best course of action if the posse did show up, he asked himself. Glancing toward the door he entered, it occurred to him that he should block that door from the inside, forcing any curious searcher to enter the barn through the front. They would have to open the large door, then stand and stare into the dark interior, which would make them reluctant to start inside and, if they did, would make them clear targets.

It was when he began looking about for some sort of heavy implement to block the door that he smelled smoke. He stopped instantly, exhaling and then inhaling to make sure he was not imagining it. Smoke.

"Oh my god. How can it be that the one barn in all of Texas I choose to hide in is on fire?"

Instantly his thoughts departed from finding a way to block the back door and turned to finding the fire in the barn. The smell, though distinct, was faint. Perhaps the fire was not large and, despite the abundant fuel in the wooden, hay-filled structure, he could extinguish it. An image of the barn afire, the smoke summoning attention from farms and settlements for miles around, seized him.

Quickly he moved through the dark, cool lower level of the barn and found nothing. He gazed up. The smell of smoke had to be coming from the hayloft. He clambered up the ladder to the loft that spanned the entire interior of the barn. Dusty slivers of sunlight leaked through the wooden slat walls, revealing hay piled in stacks of various heights. The smoke, still not visible, seemed to be coming from one spot where the bales were stacked high with a lower central core, like a small valley of hay.

He scooted across the bales on his hands and knees, the smell of smoke growing clearer as he did, until he perched above the depressed area of hay and gazed down upon—a half-grown girl. He gasped in surprise at the sight of her and she gasped upon seeing him. Fourteen or fifteen, wearing a faded cotton dress that revealed her legs and bare feet as she lay on the floor of the loft, she stared back at him. He knew she had heard him, probably everything he had said, from the time he entered the barn. She had listened to him in silence as he unsaddled his horse and scrambled through the barn searching for the source of the smoke.

The smoke? The fire? In her hands he saw a length of twisted vine and lying beside her a handful of matches.

He sighed, suddenly relieved, and then angry.

"Little sister, you've been smoking grapevine."

He gazed at her. She was pretty, her wide eyes blue or perhaps green—he could not tell in the dull light. Her hair was the lightest shade of brown and tied behind her head.

He shook his head and said quietly. "What the hell are you thinking? Do you not know this barn is nothing but a tinderbox, just waiting for a match to turn it into a big old campfire?" When she did not respond, he said, "There's a creek behind the barn not 200 yards where you could smoke to your heart's content."

3

"There's copperheads and moccasins around the creek," the girl said quickly, not so frightened or cowed as he had thought.

"So climb a tree," he said. He gazed around the loft, his thoughts returning to securing the barn from the posse that might come upon the farm at any time. "I have half a mind to tell your daddy what you've been doing. He'll give you the licking you've got coming."

He crawled away from the girl back toward the ladder that led to the lower level of the barn. There was a hay door on both the back and front walls of the barn and he began to make his way to the back to check the trail from which he ridden to the farm.

"This is not my daddy's barn," the girl said. She emerged from the depression in the hay and watched him. She kept her voice low. "My pa and ma are dead. This is my Uncle George's farm. And I don't love him."

"Well, he don't want his barn burned neither, sis. That's why you kept so quiet when I come in. You thought I was him and you had a licking coming."

He looked back to make she wasn't carrying a lit grapevine and saw her smile, bold and girlish.

Tilting her head to the side, she asked, "Who are you anyway? Why are you hiding your horse in here and sneaking around in folks' barns?"

"None of your sassy business, missy."

"My name is Callie. What's your name?"

He undid the wired latch and opened the hay door only enough to see the dirt path leading to the woods. He felt the girl draw to within a few feet of him. She was looking over his shoulder, trying to see what it was he was watching for.

"My name is cowboy-passing-through-mind-your-own-business."

Though she kept her voice low, it had a joyous, playful lilt to it. "Didn't I hear you say something to your horse about people following you? . . . Like a bunch of men, didn't you say?"

He glanced back at her, annoyed. "You just need to hush."

"Or what? Who are these fellows a chasing you? Are they, maybe, a posse?" She waited for his reply and, when he didn't speak, she said. "That trail from the creek to the house leads up from the direction of Commerce. They have a bank in Commerce. . . . I bet you robbed it." She gasped. "I know who you are."

He turned to her, his face dark and impatient. "No you don't."

"Yes I do. I bet you're Richmond Booe, the bank robber."

He turned back to the hay door. "No."

"Ha! Yes, you are."

"I'm the preacher Brother Jones. I'm running from some boys for marrying their sister to their reprobate cousin."

She giggled. "You are Richmond Booe. Hiding out from the law in my uncle's barn."

He started. "Ought oh."

Riders began to emerge from the woods. He counted three, five, six of them. Six. There had been a dozen or so in the posse. That's how they caught up with him. Half had taken one branch of the creek and half the other, leading six of them to the farm.

They sat on their horses in the clearing, staring at the farmhouse and the barn. They were discussing, he knew, what they should do next. They were debating whether or not to enter the barn or surround it. Or should they check out the farmhouse itself? They were wondering if he might have hidden his horse in the barn or the woods and then got himself in the house, perhaps taking the family within it as hostages. Or the farm might have been too obvious and dangerous a place for him to stop and they might be wasting time looking for him here if he had already ridden north. Silently they spread in two directions, riding around the barn slowly and making their way toward the house.

5

"Callie," he said softly, "is that what you said your name is? Here's what you're going to do and I ain't telling you this but once. You're going to stay right here, laying on top of two hay bales with a stack of bales all around you. And don't raise your head above the highest bale."

"Well this ain't alfalfa," she said tartly, mocking his tone. "You really think it'll stop a .45 slug?"

"You better hope it will."

He crawled as swiftly and quietly as he could toward the hay door on the front wall of the barn. Halfway there he realized the girl was following him. Booe looked back at her face, her eyes wide with excitement.

"She's going to get us both killed," he muttered. He looked back and whispered, "You sure listen good, don't you?"

Turning the wooden latch on the hay door, Booe pushed it out just far enough to be able to see the front porch of the house from the opening. Lowering his eyes to the door frame, he could see either side of the barn and watched in stillness as all six of the riders came into view and stopped before the front of the farmhouse. They were jittery, most of them turning from the house to the barn and back. None had drawn weapons, but their hands were atop their pistols and rifles.

"Hello in the house!"

It was the tallest, oldest rider. Booe has seen him following at a distance when the posse fell in behind him twelve or fifteen miles north of Commerce. He wore a tie and had a badge pinned on his suitcoat. This lawman was in charge of the posse and, Booe assumed, the others would do as he told them.

One rider—young and seemingly very eager—caught Booe's attention. His hand on his holstered pistol, he kept his horse in constant motion, turning back and forth in front of the barn, gazing down each side. If gunfire erupted, this would be the first person who would draw and shoot.

The front door of the farmhouse opened and a stout, dark-haired man in his early forties stepped onto the porch. Following behind in meek silence was a woman, thin and dressed in the same sort of faded dress the girl was wearing. The two stared at the horsemen prancing back and forth before them.

"Name is Sheriff Pope, mister. Sorry to disturb you so close to suppertime, but the bank was robbed in Commerce today and we've tracked the robber to your property here." The sheriff gazed at their faces, trying to gauge their fearfulness, to determine if someone might be behind them with a gun pointed at their backs. "Wondered if you've seen any fellers come round this way who don't belong?"

"Nope," the farmer declared simply.

"We're going to check your barn," the young, excitable rider said.

"No you're not," the farmer said, his tone calm and determined.

The cowboy turned his horse and came closer to the porch. "You got a back door to this barn, mister. He could have snuck in without you knowing."

Booe shook his head and whispered, "You're the first one I'm going to gun, puppy."

"No he couldn't," the farmer said. "I been sitting in the front room doing books all afternoon. If somebody come out of those woods, I'd of seen 'im for sure. I saw you boys coming up the trail the minute you busted out of the trees."

The sheriff nodded. "Of course—I didn't catch your name, sir."

"Rushing. George Rushing. This here's my wife Naomi."

"Well, Mr. Rushing, of course there's six of us and we aren't trying to be stealthy. We're just looking for one man and he's got reason to sneak about slyly, like my deputy said."

Booe felt the girl kneeling beside him, looking over his shoulder, her thick hair brushing his face.

On the porch, her uncle was shaking his head. "Nothing happens on this farm without me knowing," he said. "Coyotes come up and I know they're here before they ever commence to howling."

The girl snickered. "Uncle is a fool. He don't know half the stuff transpires right under his nose."

Booe slid the Peacemaker in his left hand into its holster and lifted his index finger to his lips. Barely audibly came his, "Shh."

"Mr. Rushing," the sheriff persisted, "have you any creatures about that might have made noises of alarm in the last few minutes? Maybe a hound dog a barking?"

Rushing put his hands on his hips. "Ain't got a dog. Had one and shot him a couple months ago for killing chickens."

Booe felt the girl tense beside him. "That wasn't his dog, it was my dog," she whispered angrily. "And he didn't kill chickens. He killed a rooster what wouldn't stop pestering him."

Slowly Booe raised his hand and covered the girl's mouth. Their faces a scant half foot apart, he stared in her eyes. He let her go and took the Colt back into his hand.

"I don't see why you'd be so touchy about letting us walk through your barn," the young rider said, his voice accusatory. "After all, we're the law."

Leaning his head back, his expression defiant, Rushing said, "Because keeping out of my barn and off my property is the law, son. The big law of this land says I don't have to let you onto or into my property, less you got a warrant. Now do any of you fellows have a warrant to search my barn?"

"When you're chasing a bank robber who's only half a mile ahead of you, Mr. Rushing," the sheriff said, "you generally don't have time to fetch a warrant. To be sure, we are only asking for your cooperation. I'd like to think you wouldn't mind giving us that."

"I brook no concord with no bank robber," the farmer said. "Still, as I told you, I would surely have seen a stranger

8

and there ain't been one. The way I see it, you're wasting your time lingering here while you let him slip away."

"Mister," the young man said, "give me one minute to walk through your barn and we'll be on our way."

Booe could see that George Rushing, despite his prideful assertion no outsider had been near his farm that day, was seriously thinking of letting the posse examine his barn. Letting go of the inside of the hay gate, Booe touched the handle of his right side Peacemaker, the Quickdraw and the Buntline and the extra Colt in succession. Mentally he rehearsed the order in which he would pull the guns and at whom he would begin to fire.

In the long minute of silence, Sheriff Pope spoke up, "Besides yourself and your wife, do you have anyone else on the farm. Maybe some of your children or a field hand might have been about and seen something?"

"Just got a shiftless niece." Rushing looked over his shoulder at his wife. "She ain't in the house, is she?"

The woman shrugged. "No."

Rushing filled his lungs with air and bellowed, "Callie! Where are you?"

The girl grabbed Booe's arm, pulling him back from the hay gate and pushing it open. Booe's immediate inclination was to throw her back into the hay, but before he could do anything she answered her uncle loudly.

"Uncle George? I'm up here. What are y'all doing?"

Booe positioned himself back from the window, a Peacemaker in each hand, the hammers locked back into firing position. He could see all the riders turn in their saddles, looking up at the girl, whose head and shoulders protruded from the hay gate.

"What are you doing in the loft?" her uncle asked.

"Cat had her kittens and I was up here watching."

"Well you don't need to be up there when you should be down here helping your aunt fix supper."

"Yes, sir."

"Young lady," the sheriff said, "how long have you been up there in the barn?"

"Oh I don't know," she said. "About an hour, I guess."

"We're looking for a feller who might have passed through a few minutes ago."

"A cowboy?" she asked. "You mean a man with a long coat on a dark red horse?"

The posse riders wheeled their horses to face her, entirely focused on her words.

"Where did you see him?" the sheriff asked.

"I heard him coming out of the woods about ten minutes before I heard y'all. I crawled back to the back door of the hayloft and looked out the window. He went yonder, the long way around the house up the north trail." She pointed toward the pathway a quarter mile from the farmhouse.

Instantly everyone in the posse except the sheriff reined their horses toward the trail and trotted away from the barn and house. Booe felt himself breathe. Gently he lowered the hammers on the Colts and leaned back against a bale of hay.

"Thank you, miss," the sheriff said.

"Is he in trouble?" the girl asked.

"He is trouble. He's a bank robber and a dangerous man. Before today he's kilt people while robbing banks and making his getaways."

"Get down out that loft and come help your aunt now."

"Yes, sir. One of the kittens was born dead and I thought I'd take it out and bury it behind the barn rather than coming right down, if that's okay."

Rushing grimaced. "Lord, yes. Get it out of the barn whatever you do."

"Okay, Uncle. I'll be in directly."

She pulled the wooden gate inward. Booe, who had holstered his Colts, caught the door and held it open just enough that he could see and hear the sheriff, who still sat on his horse, talking to the farmer.

"Much obliged for your help," the sheriff said.

10

"Glad to help, such as it was." The farmer tilted his head. "You say this robber is a killer and a dangerous fellow. Sounds like you know who he is."

"Yes sir. Richmond Booe, if I'm not mistaken."

Rushing's mouth feel open for an instant. "Do tell. Richmond Booe. Well . . ."

The sheriff tightened his reins and turned his horse in the direction of those who had ridden on before him.

"I'd wish you luck, Sheriff, but I'm not sure whether good luck means catching up with Booe or not catching up with him."

"If'n I do catch him, we'll be shooting forwards and he'll be shooting backwards. That's about all I got going for me."

"That one hot-headed deputy of yours is just itching for a fight."

"Yeah, I'd put him at the back of the pack, but he'd shoot right through the middle of us. I figure Booe'll shoot him and then maybe we'll shoot Booe."

"You got him, by the numbers."

The sheriff spurred his horse and, looking over his shoulder at Rushing, said, "Yeah. Had a dozen before we split up. Hope we have enough firepower. Booe's a hard man to kill." He touched the brim of his hat. "Good day to you."

"And to you. If you get him, bring him back through so we can see his body."

When the sheriff was out of earshot, the farmer turned to the door of the farmhouse and nodded. He went through the front door, followed silently by his wife.

Booe sighed. He closed and latched the hay door and looked at the girl.

"Callie's your name. I reckon I owe you. That was quick thinking there. Saved a for-sure gunfight."

She stared at him. She was, Booe recognized, unusually lovely. And behind her eyes—which were bright green— there was mischief and cleverness.

"I didn't do it so much for you as for those deputies."

11

"You don't say."

"You were about to shoot them all."

". . . If I had to."

"You had a plan in mind, didn't you?"

He nodded almost imperceptibly. "The two at either end of the barn were going down first, so they couldn't flank me. Then the big mouthed kid, mostly because he was going to fill the air with lead. The other three would've been right in front of me and the advantage would've been mine I reckon."

They gazed at each other.

"You going to saddle up now and go?"

"Soon as I can. I need to rest my horse for another half hour or so, then I'll slip out the back way I come in. I hope that won't create no hardship for you."

"No. And you don't have to worry about Uncle George. You could sneak an army out the back of the barn and he'd never know."

"What are you going to do if that cat don't have her kittens?"

She laughed. "Uncle George don't seem to know that Little Momma had her litter the day before yesterday. And all the kittens are just fine, thank you very much."

He chuckled. "Ain't you the smart one? I had a good day banking over in Commerce. And since you engendered my escape and safety, I need to share some of the take with you."

"You mean money? Are you trying to give me some stole bank money?"

"Yep."

She shook her head. "I got no use for it. Not exactly what you'd call a shopper. Got to make my own clothes. I get to town about once every two months. And if, on some rare occasion I did get to the store, I would have no way of explaining how I got some spending money."

He considered her words. "Well, you ought to take it anyway. Don't girls your age keep a hope chest? You know, so you can invest in a wedding dress and maybe a trousseau?

Don't you need money to get ready for getting hitched?"

Her laugh was different this time, ironic. "That would be the biggest waste of all, Richmond Booe. Not much to choose from around here when it comes to marrying."

Shrugging, he said, "Well. You're a pretty gal. You ought to have your pick."

"My reputation is that I have a smart mouth. I say what I think and I don't take orders. I've also let on that I can't cook, which suits my purposes."

"Yeah, you're a sly one, sis. Still, you have to think about your future. Be smart, I say. Pick out a fellow who has some land and ain't prone to hitting womenfolk. Somebody who loves work and is good at farming. It don't matter how good-looking he is once the sun goes down, you know."

She gave him a little smirk. "Thank you for that good advice, Richmond Booe. If robbing banks dries up, you can commence to giving romance tips."

He laughed.

"I'm going down and help Aunt Naomi fix supper. And I'll keep my aunt and uncle out of the barn for next hour or so." She rose slowly and crawled to the ladder.

"You know where I hid my saddle?"

She stopped, only her head visible to him. "Yeah?"

"Don't let nobody else look under that pile of hay before you do."

Her eyebrows arched. "I told you not to leave any money."

"If you don't want it, you better decide who to give it to. Or maybe hide it away for some future day. Nobody can tell from looking at it where it came from."

She stared at him, but did not speak again.

He heard her descend the ladder, open the barn door and latch it again. He swung the hay gate inward just enough to see her walk across the yard and up the steps to the porch. Just before she disappeared into the house, she glanced over her shoulder at the loft.

Chapter 2
Holiday Wedding

The young black man was singing a spiritual. The words and melody rhythmically kept time with his shovel as he plunged it into the dirt of the potato field, turned the earth and repeated his motion.

He was so caught up in his labor and the words of the hymn that he did not hear the rider emerge from the thicket behind him and walk his horse slowly to within a dozen feet of the singer. The cowboy sat, listening.

". . . and I ain't got no home—in this world anymore . . ."

The pony shifted its weight and the saddle creaked softly. The farmer turned abruptly and just as swiftly shielded his eyes from the late morning autumn sun. The rider had approached with the sunlight directly behind him, so all the singer could see was the outline of a man astride a horse clad in a duster with a broad brimmed hat. Reflexively, he gripped his shovel, lifted it and took a step to his left, trying to see some detail of the stranger's face.

"Mornin', Cap'n. Reckon I didn't hear you ride up."

The rider laughed, his shoulders moving slightly. "You don't recognize me, do you, Jeremiah?"

He let the wooden handle slide through his fingers. "Richmond? Is that you?"

Sliding his hat back on his head, the cowboy leaned forward. "Tell me something, Jeremiah. Do you know any other human being stupid enough to claim to be me?"

"Well it is you. Alive and in the flesh. Richmond Booe. Bank robber and gunslinger."

Richmond looked around the meadow, something he had done at length before he emerged from the woods.

"What are you doing here, Richmond?"

14

His eyes dropped to the young farmer. "I come for you, Jeremiah. Ma sent me to fetch you."

"What?"

"Is this your mule back here?"

"Well, yes."

"Come on, then." Richmond reined his pony toward the narrow path into the woods.

"Hold up, Richmond." Jeremiah had to trot to keep up with the horse. "What does Miss Louisa want with me?"

"Has to do with Miss Bessie."

Jeremiah stopped. "Momma?"

"C'mon."

"What about my momma?"

They were into the thicket and out of the clearing. Richmond slowed and looked back at the straggling farmer.

"I heard your mother been having apoplectic fits."

"That's right. She's had two."

"Well." Richmond swallowed. "She's had three now. Ma found her in her cabin yesterday."

Jeremiah's face was full of dread. "How is she?"

"She couldn't walk nor talk yesterday. Ma wanted to come find you, but was afraid to leave Miss Bessie. When I come in just a while ago, she give me a hug and kiss and sent me right off to find you."

"Is she going to live?" Jeremiah hurried to the mule tied beneath a cottonwood tree.

"She's some better this morning by Ma's account," Richmond said. "She still can't walk. But she can talk some. Called me by name. Seems like she can't use the one hand."

Jeremiah freed the mule and pulled himself onto its back. "Sounds like this spell was a bad one."

With one end of the rein, he popped the air between the mule's ears and at the sound the animal lurched forward.

Jeremiah studied the cowboy riding beside him. "Why you here, Richmond? Ain't you wanted?"

"Fact is I am. I'm wanted only in the state of Texas,

15

though. . . . There be six or eight surrounding territories and states where I not only ain't wanted, I'm more than welcome. Arkansas, Kansas, Missouri, Oklahoma Territory or the Indian Nations, they're always right glad to see me."

"Really?"

"Yep. Probably on account of me spending money I stole in Texas."

"What you wanted for?"

"Bank robbery, mostly."

"Mostly? Not murder?"

"Yeah, maybe."

A grin spread over Jeremiah's face. "I heard you been shot."

He nodded. "Four times. . . . You know what I learned from that?"

"What's that?"

"Third time ain't always the charm."

Jeremiah smiled. "So why'd you come back, Richmond?"

"Thanksgiving. Ain't seen my ma and my brothers in three year. Couldn't let anybody know I was coming. Had to be a surprise to all y'all."

They had come to another clearing, in the midst of which was a small, white-washed church adorned with a simple cross meant to be a steeple. Riding along the edge of the woods, they stared at the chapel. Behind it, close to the trees on the far side of the meadow, was a tiny house, equally roughhewn and similar in appearance.

Richmond glanced over his shoulder at Jeremiah. "I hear you built that church."

He smiled, his pride unmistakable.

"You did a good job, Jeremiah. You're a farmer, a builder and a pastor. You've done right well for yourself."

"Thank you, Richmond."

"Ma says you can really preach the word. How many you got coming to your church of a Sunday?"

"Spec' 'bout thirty. Most what she'll hold."

"Now who'd uh figured—thinking back to when we was kids—that of the two of us, you'd be so successful and I'd be an outlaw?"

"Well . . . truth be told, Richmond, you always was in trouble."

He laughed and leaned toward his old friend. "But I'm told you're fixing to do even better. I heard you're taking yourself a bride. This very day is the day you're supposed to marry Miss Mary Blank."

Jeremiah did not react the way Richmond expected he would. He gazed ahead at the path before them.

Curious, Richmond asked, "I guess you ain't all that excited about getting hitched, huh?"

The farmer sighed. "This is going to kill Momma. I know she's been looking forward to this. It's what's kept her going. But I can't get married today."

"Why's that, if you don't mind me asking?"

"Two reasons. Don't have nobody to do my wedding. I'm the preacher. Can't do my own wedding."

"You ain't the only preacher around here. Riding in, I passed a couple church houses."

"Well, those are white churches. Pastor at a white church won't let me and Mary come there. And he's going to want money to come here—if he'll come at all."

Richmond chuckled. "How much can it be, Jeremiah? It's a one time expense, you know."

"Well . . . that's the second reason. I done been robbed."

"Robbed? By who?"

Jeremiah struggled with his words, and emotions. "I bought this land we're on—fifty acres—from Samuel Blank, Mary's grandpa. Paid four dollars an acre. It's good bottomland. He give me the deed. Then, 'bout six weeks ago, old Mr. Blank passed over. The next week the banker man came to see me."

"Banker? You mean Horace Howard?"

"Hisself. He had a paper. Said it was a loan Samuel made using this land as collateral. Only he never paid the money back. Told me to come to his office and settle up. Since I owned the land, now I owned the debt, he said. So I went to the bank. He told me I owed him five dollars an acre. Said he put a lien on the fifty acres and he was attaching my money in his bank. I had 'bout, say, $175 in his bank. So he says he's calling the loan. I have thirty days to pay up. If I can't pay up, I lose the land plus the money he's holding."

". . . What did you say?"

"I asked him how I could'a got clear title to land when money was owed on it. That surprised him that I knew that— so I knew then he was lying. I told him everybody knows ain't no land in this county, including what his bank is on, worth no five dollars an acre. 'Bout the time our conversation got heated, in comes the sheriff."

"Clint Berry? He still the sheriff?"

"Yep. Come in with his gun drawn, waving it around like he was expecting some trouble."

Richmond nodded. "So the two of 'em in cahoots?"

"Spec' they are."

"And they're stealing your land and your money in the bank."

"And my church house and my own house—both what I built with my own hands."

Richmond reined in his sorrel pony. Surprised, Jeremiah stopped as well.

"Ma says that your family, my family and Mary Blank's family all coming for Thanksgiving supper this evening."

"That's right."

"Well tell her I'll be home before dark. I got to a little banking to do. . . . You don't have to tell her that last part."

The reinforced front door of the Silman jailhouse slowly swung open. The sheriff looked up from his desk to see Horace Howard, President of the Silman State Bank, filling the doorway and wearing an expression of great uncertainty. In the next instant the banker was stumbling forward, falling to the floor unprotected, his hands tied behind him.

Sheriff Clint Berry rose, watching Howard fall—and in the next moment was aware of something else moving swiftly toward him. He scarcely saw the pistol before it connected with the side of his head. He fell backward, stunned, against the rough, wooden wall and, before he could regain his balance, he was being slammed forward onto his desk. He heard the hammer of the revolver being locked back in firing position.

"Now you see, Clint," said a calm voice, "there's where you made your mistake. You watched Horace hit the floor. Instead, the minute he stumbled, you should've slapped iron even before you knew who pushed him. Course then I'd have just shot you."

The outlaw's gun pressed against his head, the sheriff spoke without moving. "Richmond Booe. I recognize your voice. I never figured you would chance coming back here."

"That's what I was counting on." Richmond ran his free hand over the sheriff, searching for weapons. "But ain't it always nice to get together with old friends for the holidays?"

The sheriff snorted. "Long as you're here, we're going to throw a necktie party for you."

Richmond dug a jackknife from the sheriff's pocket. Leaning his body against him, he slipped off one, then the second of the older man's boots. A tiny, two-shot pistol slid out of the right boot and clattered to the wooden floor.

"You know, I heard of a fellow who shot hisself trying to hide a derringer in his sock," Richmond observed. "Better in your boots than in your britches, I reckon."

The banker, still lying on his face, moaned.

Richmond stepped back. "Why don't you help old Horace up and the two of you get on into that open cell."

Moving slowly, warily around the desk, Berry glanced at

the outlaw for the first time. "I don't know what you got in mind, but you ain't getting away this time."

The sheriff helped the banker to his feet and into the jail's holding cell. They turned and watched the outlaw as he slammed the door and yanked the key from the latch.

Richmond stood returning their stares. "Well untie him, Clint. What the hell's wrong with you?"

Struggling with the taut rope, the sheriff replied, "What's wrong with you? What makes you think you can just come in here and assault the town's sheriff—"

"And the president of the bank," Richmond added as he stepped behind the sheriff's desk and sat down.

"You must want to die. Kidnapping is a hanging crime too, you know."

Dropping his hat on the desk, Richmond leaned back in the sheriff's chair, enjoying the creaking sound it made. "Last time I was here, Clint, you took a shot at me. This time you want to hang me. I'm beginning to think y'all don't want me around here."

"Oh you're wanted all right." The banker spoke up for the first time, grasping the bars before him. "I told you once and I'll say it again: I'll see you dead, Richmond Booe."

Ignoring his prisoners, Richmond put his feet up on the desk and opened the bottom drawer. He pulled out a mason jar full of amber liquid. The instant he uncapped it, a sweet, acrid odor permeated the entire room. He closed the jar quickly, his eyes fluttering.

"Is this some of Carl Clodfelter's hooch, Sheriff?" He displayed the jar. "You'll go blind drinking this, you know." Setting the whiskey back in the bottom drawer, he stretched casually. "For the health and safety of this whole county, instead of skimming money and booze from the fella, why don't you shut down his still? As much as you two steal around here, you can afford to buy some decent liquor at least."

"What is it you want, Booe?" Howard asked, a slight

20

tremor in his voice. "You want something from us. Else we wouldn't still be living."

A Colt Peacemaker slid effortlessly from his gun belt, pointed between the banker's eyes. "When you was a kid, didn't you ever tease a poison snake before you kilt it?"

Both men in the cell stepped back from the bars. Richmond holstered the gun. Reaching into the pockets of his duster, he began to produce bound stacks of money and place them on the sheriff's desk.

"That's another thing, Clint. You are one miserable excuse for a lawman. I spent seven or eight minutes next door cleaning out all the folding money from Horace's bank, and you never even knew it."

His voice angry, defensive, the sheriff replied, "This is Thanksgiving. Bank's supposed to be closed."

"Well, yeah. I'll concede that. But you and I both know that Horace likes to spend time with his money. Even on the holidays. I wasn't surprised he was inside the bank. Are you? You know, Horace, having all the money in the county doesn't qualify you to be a banker. Any more than having a gun and being a thug qualifies Clint to be the sheriff."

He arranged the money on the desk, gazing at the labels on each bundle. Then he leaned back in the creaky wooden chair, a smile spreading over his face as he gazed at the two men.

"Well, Horace, looks like I have 'bout $2700, here."

"It's not yours."

"Oh. It's not? Well come take it back." He waited for the reality of their circumstances to settle upon them. "The truth is, Mr. Banker, this has been a good year for me." He nodded at the cash piled before him. "I don't need the money. Under the right circumstances, you can have it back."

". . . What circumstances?"

Richmond pulled a parchment document from this vest pocket. "First, we're going to burn this."

A wary expression on his face, the banker asked, "What is that?"

"This is the make-believe loan between your bank and Samuel Blank. The loan you tried to foist onto Jeremiah Freeman."

"That's a proper legal doc—"

The .45 wheeled swiftly from the holster again, pointed at Horace Howard. The banker shook at the suddenness of it.

"This Colt can tell whether or not somebody is telling the truth. If somebody tells a lie, it shoots in the direction of the liar." He placed the pistol gently on the desk. "You fabricated this loan. You got the sheriff here to witness it. You stole Jeremiah's money to subscribe it. Now we're going to burn it like it never existed. Cause, truth be told, it never did."

He struck a match and held it to the lower edge of the contract. The fire, a brighter shade of yellow than the paper, climbed upward until Richmond dropped it to the floor.

The banker's voice was subdued as he watched the parchment become cinder. "How did you find that?"

"Really now, Horace. Do you think it takes me eight minutes to rob a bank? Most of that time, while you was tied up on the floor, I was looking for this. Now let's talk about this here money. I'm going to let y'all decide what happens to it. Choice number one: While you're locked up and I take this money and ride from one end of town to the other and all the while it'll be snowing dollar bills. Tens. Hundreds. You'll never know who got it. Choice number two: I leave the money in the bottom drawer of this desk and the two of you in there. I lock the jail when I leave. Tomorrow morning Jeremiah will show up with the key and let you out. Then, the next time he comes to do some banking, he'll find out that he has $500 in his account. . . . A little wedding present, courtesy of the banker who tried to steal his farm."

Still defiant, the sheriff asked, "What if we choose neither?"

"Oh," the outlaw said. "Then you get choice number three: I shut the money in this drawer and lock the jailhouse and leave y'all in there. But first I'll tip over yonder kerosene lamp and strike a match. That way you both get to die with a friend in the presence of what you love most—stole money. . . . What'll it be, boys?"

"All right. I'll give Jeremiah the $500."

"Say it, Horace. 'Choice number two.'"

". . . All right. Choice two."

"Sheriff?"

His voice was hoarse. "Two. Choice two."

Richmond slid the money into the bottom drawer. He stood, holstered his weapon and put on his hat.

"You made the wise decision boys. If y'all try to go back on it, you know I'll find out. I'll come back. And if I do, there won't be any choices to make."

It seemed to Richmond that, for a joyful occasion, the parson was too serious. Despite the pinched and put-upon expression he wore, however, the preacher was at least doing the job right.

". . . and do you, Mary Ester Blank, take Jeremiah Freeman to be your husband, to have and hold, for better or worse, for richer or poorer, in sickness and in health . . ."

In the midst of the minister's droning, it occurred to Richmond that he could've cleaned out a bank twice in the time it took to get married once. He made certain, however, that his countenance bore no expression but a happy smile. At the length the religious prescriptions seemed to be coming to an end.

". . . I pronounce that they are husband and wife together, in the name of the Father and the Son and the Holy Ghost. Those whom God hath joined together, let not man put asunder."

The parson closed the little black book in this hand, the slightest bit of relief in his expression, and gazed at the lovely young couple before him, who returned his look with delighted anticipation. Richmond leaned close to the preacher's ear and uttered a single word.

"Oh, my, of course," the parson said. "How could I forget that? You may kiss the bride."

As Jeremiah leaned forward to embrace his new wife, the two dozen people in Louisa Booe's living room erupted with shouts and laughter. An irresistible smile on his face, Richmond stood for a time in silence watching the celebration: children and adults embracing one another, tears flowing, laughter rolling through them in waves.

The preacher drew close to him and said something. Richmond had to lean down to hear what he was saying.

"Are you through with me, then?"

"Sure parson. Let's go out on the front porch."

Outside in the descending twilight, it was much quieter.

"Well, Brother Meade, I'm pleased you changed your mind and agreed to delay your own Thanksgiving supper so you could come out to my mother's and do this wedding."

The minister glanced anxiously at the pistol Richmond had not taken off his hip—even for the ceremony. "To be completely honest, Mr. Booe, in a shotgun wedding it usually not the preacher who's got a gun pointed at him."

"Course not," Richmond said. "But like I told you, I want to make it worth your while." He felt inside his hip pocket. "What's the going rate in your church for weddings?"

"My parishioners always give me $10 for conducting a ceremony."

"Ten! Parson, you and I both know half the folks down at your place can't afford five, let alone ten." He flipped him a coin toward him that shone gold in the dull light. "Here's a $20 piece for your trouble."

The minister held it in his palm and studied it warily. "Don't know if you've heard, Mr. Booe, but there's a rumor about that the bank president and the town sheriff have been locked in the city jail and that the bank has been robbed. I trust this money has not come from such an unseemly source."

"Perish the thought, parson. You of all people ought to know not to believe rumors and gossip." He leaned forward conspiratorially. "But just so's you'll know, all the money stolen from the bank was returned. And besides, it was all folding money."

"Ah." The preacher tucked the coin into his vest pocket. "I'll be off then to see if my wife wisely saved me some supper."

Richmond watched the parson untie his horse and pull himself onto the saddle. "Happy Thanksgiving to you, Parson."

As the minister rode away, Richmond heard steps along the wrap around porch. His hand automatically covered the revolver at his hip. His older brother, Tory, stopped short when he saw him.

"You missed the wedding," Richmond said.

"Meant to. Wasn't in the right mood. Didn't want to spoil the festivities."

"I guess Ma will be serving supper soon."

Tory studied his younger brother. "If you really cared about Ma and the rest of us, you wouldn't of come back here, Richmond. You brought danger with you."

"Glad to see you too, big brother. Before y'all turn in tonight, I'll be gone. And you'll have your safety back."

"It's nothing against you personal, Richmond. It's just that you can't never—"

"I understand, Tory. You don't have to say more." He looked off into the twilight.

There was the sound of the door opening and closing as Tory went in. Then it opened and closed again. Somehow he knew Jeremiah had come out looking for him.

"Hey, Richmond!"

"Hey, yourself, you old married man."

"Your momma says it's time to eat in about five minutes. Forrest is a slicing the smoked turkey he shot down by the cottonwoods."

"Well I'm ready now. Don't know if I can make it another five minutes."

Jeremiah took his place beside Richmond, leaning against the porch railing and looking out into the growing darkness. "Is it safe for you to be out here like this?"

"Safe as it gets. No cover out here for a quarter mile. Somebody's going to bushwhack me here, they'd have to come up from behind the house by the barn."

"You should've been in the house one minute ago. My momma stood up and put her arms around my new wife. They was both crying and laughing and praising the Lord." Jeremiah sounded as if he were close to tears himself. "Momma says she's looking for you. She knows this wedding day would not have come had it not been for you. She says she wants to tell Richmond Booe he did a good thing."

He laughed. "I guess does sort of surprise folks."

"No it don't," Jeremiah said. "All you done today . . . Richmond, I'll never forget it."

"Well, if that's the case, I sure hope the marriage works out."

Jeremiah laughed. "First baby we have, I'm a name it Richmond."

"Really?"

"Yep."

"Well then I hope it's not a girl."

They laughed. And when neither spoke for a time, they looked at each other.

"Why did you do that at the jail, Richmond? You coulda got yourself kilt."

"It's what a brother does for his brother." When he saw the flicker of surprise move across Jeremiah's face, he continued. "Ma didn't tell me. I figured it out from what she said about your pa." He gazed across the meadow. "Reckon I was sixteen or so. War had been over for seven or eight years. I said to her one day, 'Jeremiah's pa must've been real

26

stout on getting his freedom. Else he wouldn't have run off to enlist with the bluebellies.' Then Ma just said, 'Reckon Elwood wouldn't have run off if your pa hadn't messed with his wife.'

"I got to studying on that, Jeremiah. Gradually a lot of things began to make sense. Your ma only had one child—you. My ma had five kids—all boys. After the war was over, and it was just Ma and the three youngest of us left, and Ma wanted to come from Mississippi here to homestead, I couldn't understand why your ma would want to bring you and come with us. Why would Miss Bessie build a cabin behind our house and be like family to us?

"What made it make sense was when it come to me that your Pa couldn't father no kids. My Pap was the one threw all boys. So Pap had a child by Miss Bessie—you. I imagine that didn't sit to well with Bessie's husband. But being Pap owned 'em both, what could he do? Then along come the war. Elwood run off to join the Union. He got kilt. My Pa and the two brothers old enough to fight got kilt. That left Tory, me and Forrest. And of course you, Bessie's only child, my half-brother. That's why your Ma followed my ma here, so we brothers wouldn't be separated growing up." He looked at Jeremiah. "You know this all, don't you?"

Jeremiah nodded. "Spec' we the only two of the lot what does."

Richmond considered his words carefully. "Jeremiah, one day something is going to happen to me. When it does and the word gets back here, I'd appreciate it if you'd come fetch me home. Have 'em wrap me up and salt me down. I ought to last that way if the trip's not too long. I want you to bury me by the pond. And I want you to say the words. . . . Promise?"

". . . You know I will, brother."

"Well, let's go celebrate Thanksgiving. While we can."

27

Chapter 3
A Professional Invitation

At first Booe assumed that the auburn-haired girl in the flowing green formal gown with the yellow parasol on her arm—who had previously escorted him several times from the dining room of the Virginia Plantation restaurant through the narrow labyrinthine hallway to the leisure area in the adjacent building—had forgotten who he was, that he had visited the establishment before. Yet when she presented him to Darnell, the very large black man wearing a butler's cutaway coat, cravat and striped pants, she did not hesitate to announce him properly.

"Darnell, this is Mr. Richmond Booe from the Oklahoma Territory. He has been our guest previously."

"Yes, Miss Anabelle, I remember Mr. Booe."

The girl turned to leave and Darnell continued, "It's good to see you, sir. I trust you are well and that business has been prosperous."

"Thank you, Darnell," Booe replied, unbuckling his holster and handing it across the wooden counter separating them. "I'm doing just fine. And yourself?"

"I can't complain at all." He held the holster in two hands, taking care not to touch the .45 strapped in it, and placed it in wall-mounted cubbyhole. "Is this all you have to check this evening, sir?"

"Just my Colt."

"Yes sir. Your sidearm is in number 12, sir. May I ask, what sort of entertainment are you here for tonight, Mr. Booe?"

Before he could answer a woman's voice rang out. "Richmond Booe—as I live and breathe."

From the dark hallway behind Darnell a short,

28

exceedingly stout woman in a low cut red dancing dress—wearing such ample paint upon her face and baubles upon her neck, ears and fingers and radiating such an aura of strong perfume that she could never be confused with an acceptable member of society—emerged, walking toward Booe with her arms extended. She embraced him, unabashed, her full bosom pressed against him, hugging him fiercely. Then she held him at arm's length, examining him.

"Here he is, Darnell, the notorious bank robber I read about on a regular basis."

"Hello, Miss Lolly. How are you?"

She smiled as if he given her a lewd compliment. "I'm fatter and sassier than the last time you saw me, Mr. Booe. And I see you are no worse for the wear."

"I don't have any recent bullet holes in me. That's the good news, I reckon."

"Honey, you wouldn't be here at Virginia's if things hadn't been going well for you out there." She took his hand in hers.

Booe took off his Stetson with his free hand and extended it to Darnell. "You can't believe everything you read in the papers, Lolly. I hear tell I've robbed banks in little Texas and Louisiana towns I never heard of, let alone visited."

"Well you are looking vigorous, I'll say. It is so good to see you."

He nodded. "As a dear friend of mine, Mr. Bear, once remarked to me, it is better to be seen than viewed. He expired in eastern Arkansas not long ago as the result of hanging by the neck. They carried his body home to the town of Shawnee and stretched him out and I went to his funeral. I deduced from that that my friend was right. It is much better to be seen than viewed."

"Uh huh. And what brings you here this evening, Mr. Booe? You know, I don't believe you've met some of the lovely young ladies who are newly in our employ."

29

"I'm sure they can't hold a candle to you, miss. As for me, I thought I'd stop in and enjoy a bottle of good bourbon and see if anyone was playing cards tonight."

"We have several poker rooms playing this evening, sir," Darnell said. "Plus farrow and blackjack."

"No, no." Miss Lolly waved her hand. "I know just the game for my friend here, Darnell. Are those three fellows just getting started in the Wisteria Room?"

"Yes, ma'am."

She straightened his arm, forcing it between her breasts. "I have just the place for you. It's a pot limit game with some players you will find particularly interesting."

Booe looked down at her. "They aren't bankers, are they? Seems like I have a way of making bankers nervous."

"Not at all. You'll enjoy these fellows." She glanced at the man behind the counter. "Darnell, would you accompany Mr. Booe to the Wisteria Room?"

"Yes, ma'am."

She patted his hand. "You come and find me later on, if you'd like some introductions to our new sisters of leisure."

Booe knew not to bend down, else she would have kissed him. "Thank you for that, Miss Lolly. I doubt I'll have any money left at the end of the game, however."

She waved a hand at him as she turned and walked toward the dining hall end of the complex. "Richmond Booe, your credit is ample with me, darlin'."

Wordlessly Darnell started down the dark hallway, lined with narrow doors. His shoulders nearly brushed either side as he walked. Booe followed two steps behind.

"You know, Darnell, with them striped britches and that cutaway coat, you sort of look like a preacher."

A deep chuckling sound came from the black man's chest. "And when were you last in the presence of a preacher, Mr. Booe?"

"Actually I kidnapped one at gunpoint a couple months ago."

"Do tell."

"I needed him to do a wedding for my brother and his girl. He proved somewhat reluctant and additional persuasion was necessary."

Darnell turned a corner and continued down a second hall. "He didn't want to conduct a free wedding, sir?"

"No. The preacher was a white man. . . . My brother, on the other hand, is just a bit darker than you."

Darnell's head jerked quickly to the side and he glanced over his shoulder. It was the first movement Booe had ever seen from him that wasn't deliberate and measured.

They stopped in front of a white door with the word "Wisteria" painted on it in blue. Darnell eyed Booe curiously as he opened the door and nodded to his guest.

The three men sitting around the felt-topped table looked up simultaneously at the opening door. As was his learned custom, Booe studied them quickly before stepping into the room. One, somewhat dishelved with a jacket over a brocade vest, was obviously inebriated. He was stubble-faced and wore a belligerent expression. Booe judged him immediately to be a hothead. A second man, wearing a tailored jacket, was observing Booe with an equally keen eye. He was lean and had sharp features. Booe guessed him to be in his early 30s, and thought, with his thick, dark hair, mustache and narrowly trimmed goatee, that this very observant fellow looked like a plantation owner. The third man, older and heavier than the others—and much more relaxed, seemed familiar to Booe. He too was nicely dressed. He seemed to recognize Booe as well and smiled broadly.

"Gentlemen," Darnell said, "as you are just getting started, Miss Lolly has asked you to welcome another player to your table."

"Come in, friend," the older man said.

Darnell pulled out a chair for Booe directly across from the drunken player. Being careful not to call Booe by name, he said, "I'll send Trixie in directly with your bourbon, sir.

31

Do let me know if you require anything else."

"Thank you, Darnell."

After the door closed, the four men sat about the table silently. The thin, mustached man, unhurried, shuffled a deck of poker cards. Two kerosene lamps sat at in corners of the room, illuminating mostly the ornate wallpaper.

"You fellers just getting started?"

"I won the deal by virtue of high card," the thin man said. "Just about to deal the first hand." He tossed a white poker chip to the center of the table. "Dollar ante for seven card stud."

Booe pulled a small, folded bundle of bills from the inside pocket of his jacket and, holding the money below the table, counted out $50. "What's the buy in?"

"Blue chips are ten. Red are five. Whites are one. Buy in for whatever you can stand to lose. The bank is in front of that empty seat."

The dealer waited until Booe had purchased his chips, then began shucking cards. Booe's first three cards were all hearts, with the five of hearts showing. The hand progressed smoothly. Booe's fourth card was a spade, but the fifth was the ace of hearts. The inebriated man, who had a pair of kings showing, began to bet heavily. Booe called each of his bets, but did not raise. His sixth card, the last upturned card, was also a spade, a king. The dealer and the older man folded their hands, leaving only Booe and the drunk—who bet $20 in an attempt to scare him into folding. Booe called.

"Down and dirty, gentleman." The dealer had a distinctive soft southern accent.

The seventh card slid across the table face down. Booe glanced at it quickly: the nine of hearts. Then he looked at the drunkard's hand. It was possible the fellow might have a full house, but he had started raising the bet before he pulled his last three cards. Chances were he had another king—but no more than three because Booe had the fourth. His opponent bet another $20 and Booe called.

32

"Three big cowboys," the drunk said triumphantly.

"Doesn't beat a heart flush," Booe responded, dumping over his hole cards.

Booe let him stare at the upturned red cards for an instant before he began raking the chips toward himself. The loser's stunned silence settled into sullen anger.

"You were pretty lucky there, mister."

Booe shrugged. "Well, if you don't win the first one, you can't win 'em all."

The deal reverted to the drunken player, who was struggling to shuffle the cards just as the door popped open and a young woman in a short red dress and sheer white blouse came in. She was holding a bottle of bourbon by the neck with a shot glass turned over the top.

Focusing on Booe, she said, "Are you Mr.—"

"Mr. That's-My-Whiskey," he interrupted. "Yes I am. You must be the famous Trixie."

Her smile was girlish. She set the bottle and glass before him and said, "Miss Lolly told me to tell you she put the liquor on your bill. She told me to introduce myself to you and ask if there was anything else I could do for you."

Booe nodded. "And did she tell you how I was supposed to answer?" He fished in his hip pocket for a silver dollar.

Confusion crossed her face. "Well. No."

"And I thought she had this all figured out." He handed her the coin. "Here's for your trouble Miss Trixie."

The girlish smile returned. "Oh! Thank you." She looked at him slyly. "Maybe I'll see you later."

"I don't know, girl. These fellows are cleaning me out. That there was my last dollar."

"Oh. Oh no." Disappointment in her voice, she said, "Well, that's too bad Mr.—"

"Mr. Thanks-But-No-Thanks. Make sure you tell Miss Lolly that I said you're a right pretty girl. Second only to her."

She giggled and let herself out the door. Booe shook his

head and pulled the cork from the bottle.

The others, who had been watching in silence, laughed. The inebriated man began shuffling the cards again.

Then older man, chuckled and said, "A couple times there before you stopped her, I thought she was going to come right and call you Richmond Booe."

They exchanged looks. Booe filled his glass and corked the bottle. He sipped the hot, sweet whiskey.

"Well," he said, "you look familiar to me as well, sir, having seen your face on a few post office walls. You're Mr. Cotton Neal, if I am not mistaken. Lead man of the Kiamichi Boys—mostly train and bank hold ups. And before that— during the war, that is—you were a prominent figure among the Tennessee Volunteer regulars."

Neal listened studiously to Booe's description. He nodded and said, "Ah, Tennessee. My home state. As it happens, I am not well received there these days."

"Yep. Well, I ain't the most popular feller in Texas neither. If I was to walk into any bank in the state, no one would assume I was opening an account."

Neal tilted his head toward the thin, silent figure sitting across from him. "If I don't miss my guess, this here man has some notoriety as well. Can you guess who he is?"

Booe leaned back in his chair, looking at the intense face that looked back at him. "Based on my reading of *Uncle Tom's Cabin*, I would guess that he's Simon Legree."

The man laughed, unoffended, and stroked his thin goatee. "No relation. Though I am a child of the South and southern culture."

"I reckon we all are," Booe said. "That's why we gravitate to a place called Virginia's, where the workers are all decked out in classic plantation attire."

"Let me tell you who I think he is," Neal said, turning to the thin man. "I reckon you to be Mr. T. Jeff Scott."

Booe's jaw dropped. "Really? Are you?"

"I am," the man replied casually.

Admiration in his voice, Booe said, "Thomas Jefferson Scott of the Blue Ridge in Virginia. The shootist. . . . I trust, Mr. Scott, you are not here in Kansas City and in this fine establishment on business. Or at least not business dealings with present company."

Scott's brow furled momentarily as he reflected on Booe's question. "I am not at all here on business, Mr. Booe. In truth there is a certain young lady—well, perhaps not quite a lady—I'm here to see this evening. Her time and services, I'm told, will not be available for another few minutes. So Miss Lolly suggested that I seek the distraction of a card game while I waited." He ran a finger along the felt table top. "But to answer your broader question, I have never hunted bounties, Mr. Booe. My work is to provide the intimidation of effective firearms to those who need such assistance." He tilted his head. "At any rate, there would be no point in attempting to apprehend you, with or without a piece. My understanding is that Richmond Booe is pert near indestructible. You can shoot him and shoot him, but you can't kill him."

Booe swallowed the remains of his drink and reached for the bottle. "Not so, Mr. Scott. No one is indestructible. I am, however, quite lucky. Or, to be exact, I have been lucky. And no one knows when one's luck will expire, followed quickly by oneself." He glanced around the table, smiling. "Well I feel as if I'm in the presence of royalty. Sitting here at this table, lowly infamous bank robber that I am, I'm with the famous outlaw Cotton Neal and the legendary gun slinger T. Jeff Scott."

"What am I, then? Cold horse piss?"

They looked at the inebriated dealer, still fumbling with the cards, who had spoken.

"You have the better of me, sir," Booe said. "I regret that I do not recognize you. Though, by your apparel I would judge you to be a gentleman of means."

The drunk snorted. "I am Tibadeaux Timmons. I run the

35

assay office in Moore County, North Carolina. There is gold in North Carolina, gents. Last full year my office certified more than a quarter million in dust and nuggets. Not to mention semi-precious stones quarried from the mountains and foothills."

"Must be stressful work," Booe said, lifting the shot glass to his lips. "Seeing how you've come all the way from North Carolina to Kansas City for a holiday."

Timmons frowned. "Actually there has been some confusion in my office. Maybe a hint of irregularity involving some small portion of the monetary value of the gold we were dealing with. For some reason the imbalances were attributed to me. And I thought it best to travel the nation for a time and allow the legal authorities to sort things out on their own."

Booe sighed. "Well, as the saying goes, you can rob a man with a fountain pen easy as with a six gun. And there is a lot less chance of getting shot or hung." He pointed at Timmons with his whiskey glass. "I must say I assumed, what with that fancy embroidered vest, that you were some sort of a highfaluting funeral director. Or maybe a Republican congressman."

Timmons' back straightened. "I am no undertaker, sir, much less a Republican. I take umbrage at your offensive remark."

"Take it easy, friend," Booe responded. "I was just joshing with you and meant no insult. I knew you had to be a worthy type. After all, you've found yourself to the classiest eating establishment-dance hall-whore house-gambling parlor in all of Kansas City."

"Why don't you deal the cards," Scott said softly, "before you shuffle them spots clean off."

"I'm getting to it." Timmons' voice was indignant. "Five card stud. Dollar ante."

If Booe hadn't gotten a ten of diamonds as his hole card, followed immediately by the ten of hearts, he would have folded out of the hand just because the drunkard irritated him. As it was, he decided to stay and see another card. Timmons threw him a third ten, a club, for his next card. Since his was the only hand with a pair showing, Booe was the first to bet. He scratched his head as if struggling with his decision.

"I'll bet . . . make it three dollars."

"Five to play," Timmons said, bumping him.

From the corner of his eye Booe could see that Timmons had an ace and a seven showing. The best he could have thus far was two aces. He rubbed his chin, concealing his awareness that he knew he had the better hand.

"Well . . . all right. I call."

The bet, the raise and the false studiousness were repeated twice more. There was no pair showing higher than his tens, meaning Booe had a lock to win the hand. After Timmons raised him on the last card, Booe stared at him.

"No, Mr. Timmons. I think you're bluffing. I don't think you have anything in your hand that can beat my pair of tens. I'll call your raise and raise you back $20."

The taunt and challenge, as Booe suspected, were too much for Timmons to resist. "I'll see your raise and raise you back $20."

Wordlessly Booe tossed in his blue chips, then rolled over his hole card. "Trip tens beats two aces."

Timmons' mouth dropped open. Booe took another sip of bourbon watching his opponent wrestle with his lost hand.

Rage and disbelief in his voice, Timmons spoke tersely. "You lured me into thinking you only had a pair of tens. And all the while you knew you had the best hand at the table."

"Yep," Booe nodded solemnly, "and you fell for it."

He sat for a moment, waiting for his opponent to respond. When Timmons did not—apart from a wild, helpless look of rage in his eyes—Booe leaned across the table to pull the chips to himself. In that instant, Timmons lunged toward him, extending his right hand in which Booe saw—at the very point in which he was most extended, his weight over the table, and unable to respond—a six inch hunting knife coming toward him. The first thing that came to Booe's mind was the realization that his revolver was safely checked behind Darnell's counter. The second, equally instantaneous thought was that it wouldn't have mattered. This knife was coming for his throat and the wound was going to be deep and fatal.

Nearly in the same motion, as Timmons' thrust, from the corner of his eye Booe saw a swift, precise motion from Scott. The shootist caught Timmons' wrist in midflight and pushed his hand straight down. There was a thud as the joined force of their two hands embedded the knife in the wood beneath the felt covering of the table. And for a full two or three seconds, none of the three moved, each taking in what had happened. The next crashing sound, accompanied by the bitter, acid spray of red eye whiskey, was Neal's liquor bottle smashing against the back of Timmons' extended head. The attacker's head dropped onto the table, his mouth open in an astonishment not revealed in his half-lidded eyes.

There was again a silent moment as the three still seated around the table studied the motionless figure of Timmons, his upper body atop the felt, lying on the chips and cards, his hand still around the handle of the knife.

Booe tilted his face, watching Timmons for signs of movement. "Is he dead?"

"Strange, isn't it," Neal said, wiping the residue of whiskey from his hands onto the felt. "I would have bet money that he would have outlived us all."

The door burst open, the frame filled completely with the form of Darnell. He stood looking in at the man lying on the table, then gazed at each of the other men.

"Are you gentlemen all right?"

Producing a thin cigar and a match stick from within his jacket pocket, Scott said, "It would appear Mr. Timmons did not fully comply with the requirement that your guests surrender all their weapons."

Miss Lolly was in the doorway then, pushing her colleague to one side so she could see. Like Darnell, she did not ask what had happened.

"Gentlemen," she said, "I'm so sorry for the interruption. Darnell, would you please accompany Mr. Timmons out?"

Wordlessly the hulking man reached out a single hand, grabbed the back of the limp man's collar and, seemingly with no effort, dragged him through the door and out of sight.

"I apologize for this unpleasantness, fellows," Lolly said. "Mr. Timmons will not be patronizing the Virginia Plantation again."

"You're telling me," Booe muttered.

"Tonight the drinks are on the house."

"Thanks, Lolly. I'd take another bottle of red eye, seeing how I broke the last one over that gentleman's skull."

"No problem at all Mr. Neal. It'll be coming right up." And with that she turned and left, pulling the door shut behind her.

Booe stared after her. ". . . She was remarkably undisturbed by what happened to Mr. Timmons. As was Darnell."

"I expect there's a lot such action that takes place back here in these little rooms," Scott said slowly.

Looking at his companions and swallowing, Booe said, "Many times as I been shot at and shot, you'd figure this little incident wouldn't even register. But it sure has got my goat." He nodded. "That pig sticker was coming right at my throat and there was no manner in which I could respond, retaliate or get the hell out of the way. I reckon I owe both you boys for saving my life."

"Nope," Neal replied. "It was the remarkable quick reflexes of Mr. Scott that spared you, Booe. That bottle on the head was just an afterthought."

Scott blew a smoke ring. "Not so. I managed to steer the blade down into the table and it took him by surprise. Yet momentarily he was going to recover and come up slashing. We would've all got cut and maybe kilt." He pointed his cigar at Neal. "That whiskey bottle was the right idea just at the right time."

Booe drew a deep breath. "Well I thank you, gentlemen. And, Mr. Scott, remind me never to draw on you."

The gunslinger laughed. "In reflection, sir, I half wished I had not pulled down his hand. I would have gotten to see firsthand whether or not you are truly indestructible."

"Ha. What you'd have seen was my luck finally running out, along with most of my life's blood."

The door opened again, this time slowly. An exquisitely beautiful young woman leaned against it, one hand on the edge of the door and the other holding an ornate bathrobe closed over her breasts. She gazed in at T. Jeff Scott with a tender expression of passionate affection.

"Mr. Scott." Her voice was silky and beguiling and also had a sad, childlike quality to you. "I'm so glad you waited for me, tonight." She let go of the door and held her hand toward him. "Would you come with me now?"

Neal and Booe glanced at one another, then at their companion as he scooted his chips toward the little pile of money and pulled a few bills off the top of the stack.

"Regardless of what happened before, Mr. Scott," Booe said, "I think the most exciting part of your evening is still to come."

Nodding at her, Neal said, "What a beautiful woman you are, dear. And what exceptional taste Mr. Scott has in everything."

The girl dipped her head in deference. "Why thank you, sir."

Scott stood, dropping his cigar onto the floor and stamping it out with his boot. "Well, I have always favored fair ladies, those with blonde hair and blue eyes. This is Miss

Daphne, friends. She hails from Roanoke, only a hundred miles or so from where I originated. We enjoy getting together occasionally to commiserate over our lost childhood homes." He nodded. "It's been a pleasure."

The girl took his hand and led him from the room. Scott closed the door as he departed, leaving Booe and Neal in silence.

Booe took a deep breath and shook his head. "Well, he may be lightning quick, but I'll bet he takes his time with that pretty gal."

"I would," Neal said. He leaned back in his chair. "Well the players in our poker game seem to have dwindled by half."

"So it seems."

"Just as well." His eyes narrowed and he grinned. "I have a proposition for you, Mr. Booe."

"Do tell. Call me Richmond, if you will."

"Very well. My name is Cotton."

Booe nodded. "So what's this proposition? Does it have to do with a bank?"

"Well, kind of." He considered his words. "Why don't you think about what happened here this evening? What would have happened if Jeff Scott hadn't been here?"

"Reckon I'd be dead."

"There is that possibility." He leaned forward, his voice reflective. "Now let's take into consideration the different ways that you and I go about the same sort of work. . . . You are famously a solitary fellow, Richmond. You go into a bank by yourself with a total absence of associates."

Booe nodded. "Easier to travel quick, to surprise folks. Don't have to worry about making sure your partners don't get hurt. And you don't have to split the take."

"Uh huh. Now think about the manner in which the Kiamichi Boys proceed about robbing a bank. We come in force, usually at least five and sometimes six of us. We have backup and a well-thought out escape plan in place in case

41

things go bad. Usually we have an idea whether or not a bank or a particular train has a nice payoff in it." He straightened. "Here's my proposal. It's a sort of professional invitation. . . . I need a hand like you to throw in with us."

Booe nodded slowly. "Cause one of your fellers got bushwhacked."

"Yes," Neal said. "Jordan was a fair hand. He never killed anyone who wasn't shooting at him. Sure didn't deserve getting shot in the back by some would-be bounty hunter. That kid got his due before the sun went down, by the way. . . . Still, it leaves me a good man short. The Kiamichi Boys need somebody who knows his way around. Who won't lose his head when the lead commences to flying."

Booe chuckled. "I'm not sure I'm your man," he said. "You know I been shot up a few times already."

"Because you didn't have one of us watching your back, Richmond. But you prove my point. While you have been wounded in the course of your work, you didn't panic. You didn't give up. You didn't get yourself killed or captured."

He shrugged. "Well, your words are well taken and I am complimented by your invitation. I would say, however, that while there are benefits to your way of operating it is equally true that working alone has its pluses too. For instance, those big payoffs you all are looking for usually end up in larger banks, with more built in security. And they attract more armed guards. And those for-hire boys tend to be trigger happy. And when you spend extra time checking out a bank, you run a bigger risk that somebody is going to recognize you. Even if they don't, if you ask the wrong question while you're planning things out, a banker might figure out that a plan is unfolding and the law will lay-in-wait for you."

"Your points are well taken, Richmond. I wouldn't expect you to accept an offer like mine without pondering it. I hope you will think about it." He smiled. "I just hope you don't think about it one day too long, if you catch my meaning."

"Thank you, Cotton. I won't forget I owe you, regardless."

"Well, just in case you should want to discuss it further or you want to meet the other boys, let me tell you how to get up with us." His voice softened. "If I'm not mistaken, you have upon occasion while being pursued in Texas crossed the Red River and gone up into the Ouachita Mountains?"

"Yes. I'm familiar with the area."

"Well at the south end of the Kiamichi portion of the Ouachitas is a little outpost. Just a livery stable, post office and couple other businesses. The place is called Idabel. If you ever get over that way, go into the livery and find the blacksmith. Tell him you heard he has a white mule for sale. He'll tell you what to do from there."

Booe grinned. "Go to the blacksmith in Idabel and tell him I'm looking for a white mule. Don't see how I can forget that."

"Please do consider the invitation. Nothing about working with us would prevent you from going out on your own as well, you know."

"I do know."

Neal drew a breath. "Well. What a night this has been. Met T. Jeff Scott. Got to see him in action. Met and played cards with Richmond Booe and invited him to join my gang. . . . If Lolly ever shows up with my whiskey, I reckon I'll call it a night. What about yourself?"

"Well . . . I may see if I can locate that Trixie girl and ask her how she got such a name."

Chapter 4
The Kidnapping

Lying face down on stacked bales of hay in the loft, listening expectantly for the barn door below to open, Booe found himself reliving the robbery and shootout again and again.

It had occurred to him—as he stuffed the stacks of folding money into the burlap bag—that the robbery was going too smoothly. The teller had not stolen a glance at his eyes even once the way most bank employees did—a frightened way of judging whether or not they were in danger of being shot. And when he slipped quickly out of the bank and mounted Jack, the main street of the little town was completely deserted. Perhaps, he said to himself, he was being overly cautious. Still a feeling of suspicion gripped him as he made his way back through town the way he had ridden in ten minutes before.

He heard the buckboard before he saw it. Riding in, he recognized there was only one other sizeable street running through the town and crossing the one that brought him there. As he rode out of town he realized a wagon was rolling down that cross street toward the intersection. The instant he saw two people on the seat, both wearing long sleeved dresses and bonnets that covered their heads, he knew what was coming. The buckboard passed in front of him and was reined to an abrupt halt in the middle of the intersection, blocking Booe's route. The two in women's dresses turned toward him—both men. The driver held the reins tightly, trying to engage the brake so the wagon could not be moved, while the man beside him—foolishly on the opposite side of the driver—got halfway to his feet, lifting a shotgun and trying to swing it in Booe's direction without pointing it at his partner.

Booe slid a Peacemaker into his right hand the instant the wagon pulled in front of him and when he saw the scattergun he fired at the man holding it. The round went through the neck of the driver and hit the other man in the chest, knocking him out of the wagon to the street, the scattergun pitching forward uselessly. And at the sound of the gunshot, the half dozen men concealed in the back of the wagon pushed the canvas tarp off themselves and sat up, training their weapons on Booe and shooting. As he returned their fire, Booe felt the awful slap of being shot at least twice. He also heard bullets sizzle past his head in the air. The men were scared and were shooting wildly. For his part he was aiming dead center at each and hitting his mark with nearly every round. Only one man, his revolver empty, remained unwounded in the wagon as—driverless—it lurched and began to roll out of his way, the horses harnessed to it spooked by the blasts of the guns.

It was then Booe pitched forward, almost knocked from his saddle from behind. He heard another report and, glancing over his shoulder, saw a rifle barrel protruding from a second story window thirty yards away. He raised the Colt in his right hand and fired once in the direction of the shooter, who pulled the gun back inside the window. With the shot at the window, both .45s he held were empty. As calmly and quickly as he could, Booe holstered them and drew the spare Peacemaker from his belt. He fired twice at the window. The first round broke glass above the opening. The second went through the wood frame beneath the window and immediately there was a scream, followed by yelps of pain.

Booe spurred Jack, who was only too glad to gallop away.

The taste of brass still strong in his mouth, for the first half hour of his escape the pain of his wounds did not hinder Booe. As he rode, he went over the gunfight in his mind. There had been eight or nine shooters and he had wounded or

45

killed all but one. The chances were that the men he had shot up would have been the very men who formed the posse to chase him. He hoped it meant there were no riders in close pursuit, because he was badly hurt.

When he came a cloistered ford of a little stream, Booe dismounted to reload his pistols and to fill his canteen and to let Jack rest and drink. He had found himself tremendously thirsty and finished off his water. As he stooped and filled the canteen again, drank from it deeply and refilled it, the pain of his injuries rushed in upon him.

"Damn, Jack. I believe I'm pretty shot up. I'm think we need to go to ground for a while, even though we ain't yet far enough away."

The horse seemed to understand Booe's extreme situation. He stood still, his head lowered to Booe's chest. And in looking at the horse, Booe saw a perfectly round hole through the pony's right ear near the tip.

"Ah, Jack. I'm sorry, friend. Looks like they popped you one too." He chuckled, which became a cough and resulted in his spitting bloody sputum. "If it's any consolation, the slug that went through your ear done hit me as well." Wearily, he said, "Where shall we go to rest?"

Then, like a revelation, the memory came to him of the clever girl who had saved him almost a year before. What was her name? Callie. And where was her farm?

He pulled off his hat, estimating where he was and in what direction he would have to ride for how long to find that Texas farmhouse.

"By my reckoning, as the crow flies, that farm wouldn't be but twenty or twenty-five miles southwest of here. Which has the advantage of being in a direction no posse would assume me to take." He drew a breath he intended to be long and deep that was instead laborious and shallow, and set his hat back on his head. "Meaning no offense, Jack—'cause you are indeed a handsome example of horseflesh, holey ear and all—but if I'm soon to look upon the last face I see in

46

this life, I'd really like to see that pretty girl one more time."

Booe commenced his effort to climb onto the horse. Several times he managed to get one foot in the stirrup and pulled his weight against it, only to have to step back. Winded and light-headed, he started to sit down to rest once or twice, stopping himself with the realization that, if he sat down to rest, he likely could not get up again. At length he found a stone ledge alongside the river that was low enough to stand on but high enough to make it easier for him to get into the saddle.

"We ain't stopping now."

The ride was agonizingly slow, but devoid of human encounters. What should've taken three hours took seven and the sun had long since set by the time he happened upon the trail that led up from the creek behind George Rushing's barn. The back of the building was clearly illuminated in the moonlight and Booe rode straight toward it, glad there was no sounding of alarm from any livestock or other creature.

"I guess she didn't get her another dog," he muttered.

Inside in near total darkness, he found the well-formed paint pony in the same pen it had been in during his first visit to the barn and he led Jack into the next stall. It was brutally painful to undo the traces, slide the saddle off the sorrel pony and conceal it in the corner beneath loose hay. Once again he was tempted to sit and rest and once again recognized that he dare not stop.

He closed the gate of the stall and made his way to the ladder that led up to the hayloft. Taking one step at a time and hugging the ladder to his chest, he found the climb was not as difficult as he had assumed. Once in the loft, he paused, catching his breath and leaning against a stack of bales. Then he crawled slowly to the hollowed out place where he caught the girl smoking grapevine. A double row of bales was already high enough to serve as a bed for him. He pulled off his hat and duster and sat down on the hay and that was all he remembered until the next morning.

He had coughed and the pain shot through him wickedly, back to front. The intensity of it made his body clench and a multitude of other points of pain fired up. Booe held his breath for a time, allowing himself to relax and the sharpness of the pain to abate to the degree it would. That he was weak and weary there was no doubt. He needed at least a day just to rest, to regain his strength and to recover from the gunshots. And he was possessed of the nagging thought that he needed a doctor, a surgeon, for at least one of the wounds, the one in the back.

The dusty, early sunlight sneaking between the slats of the barn walls told him it was about 6 a.m. The farm family was surely up by now. What would happen, he wondered, if he were discovered. He was in no shape to fight and subdue George Rushing and he hoped he would not be put in the position of having to shoot him or hold him at gunpoint. The best he could hope for, he realized, was that the girl would find him first and keep her peace about there being an outlaw in the hayloft. Perhaps she would even bring him water and food. He closed his eyes and slept again.

It was, he decided, 8 or 9 a.m. when he woke the second time. It was not comfortable but at least less painful for him to lie on his stomach. The back wound from the shooter in the second story window was by far the most painful. Gradually he positioned himself on his stomach.

As he waited and hoped the girl would find him, he rehearsed the robbery and the shootout in his memory. What could he have done differently? Somehow he had been recognized as soon as he rode into town. That much should have been no surprise to him, since his likeness was on a poster in every jail in Texas. And apparently that bank had been a contingency plan in place in case someone—a known thief—came to rob the it. Otherwise they could not have mobilized such a group of well-armed men so quickly. What could he do to prevent something like this from happening again? Was it simply a professional hazard? He smiled. The first thing he had to do was survive the wounds from the previous day's gun battle.

The front door of the barn opened below and Booe heard someone enter. Almost immediately he heard the girl's voice. He remembered its lilt from the year before. She was talking to someone. No. She was singing. What was the song? It wasn't any hymn. Something about an unfaithful lover—not a song she would sing in the presence of her uncle or aunt. Booe guessed the girl was alone. She was walking toward the back of the barn where the horses were penned. Midway to the stalls, directly beneath him, she called out.

"Good morning Millie, my favorite filly. You ain't yet no mare. But I don't care."

Abruptly the girl grew silent. Booe heard the creaking of a gate. Then came the rustling sound of hay being pushed aside and the gate squeaking as it opened again. He could hear the girl's rapid steps as she came to the ladder and began to climb to the loft. She crossed the bales of hay much more nimbly and quickly than he had the night before and in an instant she was standing above him. Booe rolled onto his side to look up at her. She stared down at him with an expression of surprise and dread and some other emotion he could not quite name.

She had changed, grown, in the months since he had seen her. The girl was even prettier than he remembered. Though still not a full grown woman, her face was a bit rounder and fuller. Her thick, light brown hair was pulled back and braided behind her. She wore a different dress than the one she had worn before, but it too was faded, the dull rust color not suited to her.

After staring at him for half a minute, taking in the bloodied shirt and his pallor and helplessness, she spoke just his name. "Richmond Booe."

He smiled at her. "Hello, little sister. Long time, no see."

"How many bullet holes you got in you, Richmond Booe?"

He sighed. "Three I think. Two in the front and one in the back from a bushwhacker. That's the one troubling me." He moved slightly and waited for the stab of pain to subside. "Broke a rib, I think. Slug is still a rolling around inside of me."

"Uh huh. And is there a posse of men fixing to descend upon this farm looking for you?"

Booe shook his head. "I don't think so. I gunned the most of them who'd make up the posse and if they did get one together, they'd figure I headed northeast toward the Red River, whereas I headed southwest to get here."

She knelt beside him, gingerly pulling his shirt away from his body so she could look at his chest. "If the bullet is still in your back . . ."

"Yeah?"

"Then counting that and the four holes I see here, you been shot five times."

He chuckled, gritting his teeth. "Explains why I feel so poorly."

"You need real help, Richmond Booe."

"Well that's where you come in." He gazed at her, their faces two scant feet apart. "I was hoping you might be able to fetch me some water and some provender. I was hoping maybe you'd let me rest here for today."

"And then what?"

"And then I'll be on my way, like the last time. I'll pay you handsomely for the privilege."

She nodded. "With stole money? You foolish man. You think you'll be able to get on your horse tomorrow and ride away?"

"I have no alternative. . . . Your name is Callie, isn't it?"

She smiled.

"Well, Miss Callie, stupid as he may be your uncle is going to stumble onto the fact that he has an extra red pony in his barn here at some near point. The way I figure it, should a confrontation ensue, it would not be beneficial for either him or me."

Her tone was that of a schoolmarm chastening a foolish boy. "Richmond Booe, you need to go to the doctor. If you have a lead bullet still inside you, if you don't die from it tearing up your insides, you will get an infection straight away and maybe die from that. I can fetch the doctor, you know."

"Well that's thoughtful of you, sis. The thing is, the whole time sawbones is digging out that bullet and sewing me up, he's going to be thinking about how the $10 he'll get for healing me pales in comparison to the $1000 he'd get for turning me over to the Texas Rangers." He coughed, spitting blood onto the hay.

"Can you hold out here for another hour or two?" the girl asked.

"Reckon I can."

"Uncle and Aunt are heading out at lunch time for a social at the neighbors' five miles from here. They'll be gone all afternoon. When they go, I can bring you food and something to drink and I can clean your wounds." Her face grew firm. "And stitch the holes."

Booe stared at her in awe. "I am impressed. . . . If you are going to be messing with them bullet holes, I'd ask you a couple favors—not to impose overly on your hospitality."

A hint of a smile caressed her lips. "And what favors might those be?"

"When you come back up, I have in my saddlebags the better part of a fifth of Kentucky whiskey. That may serve as antiseptic and anesthetic, if you catch my meaning. I hope you don't have scruples against a fellow having a drink."

"Of course not. Maybe it'll keep you from wiggling when I run the needle through you."

"Right. Well, then, the other thing is a pen or pencil and some paper. Would you have that available, sis?"

"I believe so." She got to her feet. "I'll be back as soon as they leave."

"How is it that you will explain your absence at this

social, if you don't mind me asking?"

"Oh I'm not invited." Her voice was casual.

"Do tell."

"The virtue of having a quick tongue and a sassy perspective is that folks around here don't feel obliged to include me."

"I see. And you don't mind being excluded?"

"Not really, Richmond Booe."

"Well, I assume your uncle is going to come around to hitch up that filly then. Won't he see Jack?"

"Uncle George sent me out to harness Millie and bring her out. That's why I came to the barn in the first place. In fact I should be through with that now and on to my other chores."

"Well, I don't mean to get you in trouble, Miss Callie."

She cocked her head. "I am never not in trouble, Richmond Booe. See if you can sleep. I'll be back soon as I can."

The girl disappeared over the hay bales and Booe heard her step down the ladder. She went back to the stalls. He could hear her speaking to the paint as she trussed the horse to pull the wagon. Within five minutes she opened the large front door of the barn and led the horse out.

Booe's head drooped to the hay beneath him. A strange feeling welled up within him and he realized he was close to tears—not tears of sadness or fear, but of hope. The girl's willingness to help and her cleverness filled him with hope.

To his surprise, he was able to doze. Two hours later he woke to the creaking sound of a wagon rolling. He could hear it distinctly as it passed between the barn and the house and faded away.

Booe pulled himself up to a sitting position. "Let's make life a little easier on little sister," he said softly.

Making his way to the ladder, he held it tightly to his chest and started down. After a rung or two his head swam and he had to stop and wait. At length he made it to the dirt floor of the barn and found a bale of hay to sit upon near the door. Five minutes later the girl opened it and, seeing him, stopped.

"Well," she said, "that was pretty stupid, climbing down like that. But at least I don't have to carry as much up the stairs."

She brought him a plate of food: fresh tomatoes, kraut, lima beans and two pork chops. He began to eat it hungrily, then stopped part way through, suddenly nauseated.

"Drink this." The girl gave him a glass of cool milk and a piece of corn bread. "This should settle your stomach."

As he slowed his eating, she went back to Jack's stall and retrieved the bottle of bourbon whiskey. She had brought a little bundle of medical supplies with her and arranged them on seat of a wooden chair she had pulled up to where he sat. Wordlessly she unbuttoned his shirt and pulled it off first one arm and then the other as if he were a little child.

"Kind of forward, aren't you?" he asked around a mouthful of cornbread.

She stared at his wounds, her expression dark. "You better have a drink."

She was standing above him in the hayloft when he woke the next morning. Though she did not smile he could detect a lightness in her face.

"How pleased I am to see you survived my medical care, Richmond Booe. So far, at least."

"You did right good, little sister. If you get tired of being a ranch hand, you could be a for-sure nurse."

"Nurses empty bed buckets. I would rather be a doctor."

"A woman doctor?"

"A surgeon."

"And you'll give all your patients Kentucky bourbon? I'd be your first patient."

"You already were my first patient. Except I don't know what to do about that loose bullet sliding around your back."

She sat down in the hay beside him. "How do you feel?"

"Well, some better, I reckon. Got some of my strength back. I feel a little swimmy-headed. Hope you won't take it personal if I'm not my whole self."

"I'm just glad you're alive. Uncle came back from the social last night talking about the bank robbery and shootout in Bonham."

"Yeah?"

"Yeah. Turns out Mr. Richmond Booe killed two. He shot seven more, one of whom is gut shot and not expected to live."

Booe nodded. "That would be the bushwhacker. Only one I didn't have a clear shot at." He coughed and his head spun for a few seconds. "Helluva way to die, being gut shot. All that mess in your intestines spills out inside you and you get a sickness no one can cure. You fever up and die in misery."

"Uh huh. Well speaking of fevers and infections, you got one yourself." She held the back of a soft, graceful hand against his cheek. "And the cure for it is to get a doctor to take out that bullet and use a poultice to draw out the poison."

"Yes. I got that figured."

"So you want me to take you to the doctor. Or maybe bring the doctor to you?"

"No Texas doctor is going to fix me without turning me in lessen I hold a gun on him, and I can't hold a gun on him when I been chloroformed."

"Well then what is your plan, Richmond Booe?"

"Actually I do have one."

She leaned forward ever so slightly. "Seeing how you know I can keep a secret, would you be willing to share?"

"May as well. You do figure in my intentions."

"Me?"

"You." He coughed again. "Ever hear of a range off the Ouachita Mountains called the Kiamichis?"

"Up in the Indian Nations. Sure."

"There's a little town up there on the south side called Idabel. I'm going there. There's a fine feller named Cotton Neal there with a gang of outlaws like me and upon occasion they deal with such contingencies as this."

"I heard of them. The Kiamichi Boys." Callie looked past him, calculating mentally. "That's probably 100 or more miles from here."

"I reckon. Probably depends on where you cross the Red River."

"And you think you're just going to get up on your pony—feverish and weak and hardly able to stand—and ride 100 miles?"

"That's my only real option, sis."

She nodded slowly. "You're going to make some traveler very happy."

"How's that?"

"Somebody between here and Idabel is going to stumble onto your dead body along the trail and take the money you got all shot up stealing."

He laughed, which led to coughing and grimacing. "Well that's where you come in, Miss Callie."

Her eyes widened. "And how's that?"

Booe reached down beneath the bale of hay he lay on and produced the sheath of writing paper she had given him the previous day. He held several folded pages out to her. She took and opened them, squinting to see what he had written in the dull light of the loft.

"What is all this, Richmond Booe?"

He sighed. "There's a couple things there, sis. First of all, I recommend that you find a secret place—somewhere only you know about that no one could find even if they were a looking for it. Read these and memorize what you can. Then hide the pages for safe keeping."

"What have you given me?"

"Well, you ain't the only one of us who recognizes how

precarious this little journey of mine will be. And I'd like to request that you help me to remain a secret here for the rest of today to get my strength back and then I'll start out first thing in the morning."

She shook her head. "I'll do my best to keep Uncle out of the barn, the back stalls at least. But you should know it's six of one, half-a-dozen of the other as far as you holding off a day before you travel. You might get more strength back if you wait, but the fever and infection are just going to get worse. You can't ride no 100 miles sick as you are, Richmond Booe."

"That's why I give you that information, girl." He pointed at the paper she held. "When I go in the morning, I'm leaving you a couple hundred dollars. The top page is information about how to get up with my half-brother, Jeremiah Freeman. He's the preacher at a little church over near Silman. Jeremiah's mother was a slave owned by my daddy back in Mississippi. When my ma brought the family to East Texas after the war, his momma came along so as to keep Jeremiah alongside his brothers, I reckon. Jeremiah and I are the only ones figured out that we're blood kin."

He paused, gathering his breath. "Anyway, I exacted a promise from Jeremiah that, when the day come that I was found to be deceased, he would fetch my body from whatever part of the world it was in and bring it back to ma's farm. He'll say the words and see to it I'm buried where it's proper."

It seemed to him that her expression softened, that she was near to crying. He looked away, determined to finish whether she wept or not.

"Now if you should hear that someone found me lying along the trail, take that money and travel over to Silman. Give half of it to Jeremiah for him to use with whatever expenses he should encounter in the process of hauling my remains back home. If I make it to Idabel and die there, Mr. Neal will see to it that my body is returned home. Perhaps you could find a way, in that circumstance, to wire him some expense money. Fifty dollars or so."

He chanced a glance in her direction. Her bottom teeth were pressed against her top lip and tears were running down her cheeks. Nodding at the pages in her hand, he continued.

"Now if, say, I do meet my demise either here or after I get to the mountains, there's a little matter of some finances I got squirreled away. Ever hear of a town called Guthrie?"

"Yes." Her voice was muffled. "It's in Oklahoma Territory."

"Yep. There in Guthrie are three or four banks, but the largest one is called US Territorial Bank." He paused to catch his breath. "I got money in there."

"You have money in a bank?" Now her voice was incredulous.

"I do. Yes. You heard of safe deposit boxes?"

"No."

"Well if a bank is substantial it'll have a safe big enough to walk inside called a vault. And in that vault are these individual lock boxes. On that paper is the number of my box. When you go in—"

"When I go in? How am I supposed to get to Guthrie, Oklahoma Territory?"

"That's why I'm leaving you so much money, Callie. There's a train track runs right through downtown Guthrie."

"Well suppose I get to the Guthrie and I go into the bank, how do I get into your private box?"

"Go to the banker man and tell him you're my sister. . . . Or better yet, my wife. Tell him this time it was the cradle I robbed."

"I'm not that young."

"How old are you?"

"I just turned sixteen."

"Oh, you're an old-timer, you are."

"So I say I'm Mrs. Richmond Booe and he just hands over your money."

"No. You have to have the security code. It's written on the page there as well. It's the row of numbers and letters." He pointed to the papers in her hand. "Also on that sheet is a list of how I'd like the money and the property in the box divided up."

"Property?"

They looked at each other in silence. She wiped tears from her face with the back of her hand, her expression one of disbelief and impatience.

"Deeds," he said. "I've always wanted to do something for my mom and my living brothers. I knew I couldn't just up and give them money. Some bank would come around and say it was money I stole from them. So instead I've been buying land and farms in different places. My ma and brothers don't know it, but their names are each on a different deed."

The girl lifted her chin. "I can't listen to any more of this. I just hurts too bad."

"Why does it hurt? This is good news. The largest share of all this is willed to you to do with whatever you want."

"And that's another thing. You been robbing banks around here and getting shot and shot at for years. Why is it all of a sudden you want to leave this last will and testament?"

He sighed and laid his full weight on the hay beneath him. "Well. Frankly this is the worst I ever been shot up. I was close to dying. I'm still close to dying. In the back of my mind I always thought this day would come. . . . And it did." He pointed to her hands. "Now there's one more piece of paper there. In a way it's the most important."

"What is it?"

"It's a letter to my ma."

"Oh, Richmond Booe! Do you expect me to deliver a letter to your mother after you're dead?"

He nodded slowly in affirmation. "It's real important, Callie. In that there letter I explain everything about the

58

deeds and the money to her. . . . And I also tell her about you."

"Me?"

"Yeah. I tell her how you saved my life. Twice."

The girl turned her face from him. She got to her feet. Wordlessly she made her way across the uneven hay to the ladder and climbed down from the loft.

The pain of his wounds had diminished greatly, but Callie was right. The slight fever of the previous day had increased through the night. It contributed to the feeling of weakness in his limbs and prevented him from completing his preparations with his usual direct certainty. At length, through determination, he finished saddling Jack, securing his saddlebags and making sure his weapons were all loaded and in their accustomed points of access.

Before he could ease open the gate of the stall, he heard the rear barn door open.

Booe stood silently, his hand resting on the handle of the Colt on his right hip. He was too weak to fight the farmer. In fact he did not want Rushing to discover—and thus be able to report—how injured he was. News of his presence and his wounds would spread like wildfire and every fool with a gun would clog the area between Rushing's farm and the Red River. If it were George Rushing who had come through the door, Booe realized he would have to hold a gun on him and tie him up to the best of his ability. Also, he would take the pony—not to steal it, but to lead it away from the farm so Rushing would have a difficult time getting the word out about the bank robber in his barn.

He heard the slight swishing sound of worn cotton brushing back and forth and soft, feminine steps on the dirt floor and Booe relaxed. Callie's head appeared above the top rail of the gate.

"How do you feel, Richmond Booe?"

"Right well, thank you."

Her face was emotionless. "You go to hell for lying, same as robbing banks," she said. "'Course in your case, it's too late to make a difference."

He smiled. "You come to see me off, did you?"

"I did not," she replied curtly. Her head disappeared and he heard the wooden latch to the stall of the painted filly slid open.

"Well if you don't mind my asking, what are you up to?"

"I'm riding with you."

Booe stepped out of the stall and stood before the pen, watching as the girl began to prepare the horse. Her movements were crisp and certain. Clearly she had saddled the pony many times.

"Look, Miss Callie," he said slowly, "you are gracious and good-hearted. You're brave and good. . . . But I ain't letting you go with me."

"I didn't ask your permission," she said without looking at him.

"Let me say directly, you cannot ride with me."

She glanced at him. "Let me say directly, you can't tell me what I can and cannot do."

Booe shook his head. "They were right about that smart mouth, sis. Still, say what you want, I certainly can stop you from going."

She looked at him again. A clever, cynical smile flashed briefly as she asked, "You going to shoot me to stop me?"

He raised his open hands. "You yourself give me the count of those not three days past I shot and killed in Bonham. My ticket to the hanging tree was issued long ago. Shooting a knot-headed child like you will make no difference to a desperado like me."

She picked up the saddle, which was heavy for her, and slung it up to the back of the filly. Then she glanced at him. "Richmond Booe, with every bank you robbed and every posse that chased you, I don't for a minute believe you every shot at anybody you didn't expect to shoot at you."

"Sassy as you are, gunning you might be the only pleasure I've experienced at all in this trip to Texas." He paused considering his words. "But think about this, Callie. Put aside the whole notion of how I'm going to gun you and make plenty of folks happy 'cause I did. Just stop and think for a moment. What's it going to do to your life when you go riding off with an outlaw?"

The cynical look came to her face again as she cinched the saddle into place. "You mean it could be worse than it is?"

"Of course it could. How they going to treat you when you go back to school?"

"I graduated school last summer."

"At sixteen?"

"At fifteen. There was no challenge to it and no future after it." She yanked on the leather. "Uncle says there's no money to send me over to the teachers' college at Denton. . . . Can't think of anything else I want to do."

He shook his head. "Some righteous fellow around here going to come to his senses and realize what a catch you are and offer himself up to you."

"I can hardly wait for Mr. Wonderful to magically appear." She untied the reins from the gate of the stall. "I was thinking you might teach me to rob banks."

He stared at her, defeated. The idea flashed through his mind that he might brandish a pistol and point it at her, but she would realize—he knew—that he was bluffing.

It was then the barn door opened—not the large front door of the barn, but the small door at the back through which Callie had passed just moments before. Without thought he filled his right hand with a .45 and stood listening.

The loud, impatient voice of George Rushing resonated through the still air. "Callie? Are you in here?"

Booe lifted the index finger of his left hand across his lips. Callie, her mouth open and eyes wide stared at him. She, who had been so quick and certain the year before when she answered her uncle's call, was now wary, unsure. Booe shook his head.

"Dammit, Callie."

George Rushing marched forward into the part of the barn toward the animal stalls. As he appeared, Booe put his free hand on Callie's shoulder and pressed the barrel of his Colt against her temple. Her eyes widened in astonishment. Rushing glanced toward them and instantly froze, his jaw dropping. For seconds Rushing stared at Booe, who held his weapon against the girl, her face white with shock.

Finally Rushing spoke, his voice much diminished in volume and intensity. "Who are you? . . . Are you Richmond Booe?"

Booe smiled. "Your daughter here didn't have to ask. She called my name right quick."

Rushing started to speak, to correct him—Booe knew—in saying that Callie was his daughter. But he thought better of it. ". . . What do you want?"

"I done got it. I'm taking this girl and this pony."

Dismay played across Rushing's face, though he did not flinch. "That's my only horse."

This time Booe chuckled. "You more worried about this horse than your child?"

". . . Well, the girl will be of no service to you, Mr. Booe. She cannot cook, is lazy beyond proportion and has no interest in men, if you catch my meaning. You'll send her back straightaway. The horse is a different story."

"Uh-huh. Well the paint is a spare pony for me if my horse goes lame or if I have to outrun a bunch of fellers. But I'm a bank robber, not a horse thief. Wouldn't want to get hung for some matter as piddling as that. So when I get where I'm headed, I'll send the horse back, accompanied by your useless girl."

Making sure he made no overt movements, Rushing said, "Well, if she's no use to you, why not just take the horse and leave her here?"

"Well. I am surprised. That's the first gallant thing you've said, Mr.—"

"Rushing."

"Mr. Rushing. There for a while I didn't think you cared whether I kidnapped this child or not. What a pleasure to know I am mistaken. And did I hear you call her 'Smelly?'"

He felt a twinge go through the girl and resisted the urge to smile.

"Callie. Her name is Callie."

"Umm. I'm sorry to hear she can't cook. Camped out in the woods by your creek back there for the last few days, letting my wounds heal up good, I sure got a hankering for some sure enough home-cooked vittles. But frankly—" He pulled the barrel of the gun from her head and scratched his chin with the site. "—when I seen her go into the barn, I didn't see no cook nor maid servant. I seen a passport." He pointed the gun at Rushing, who shivered and seemed near to wilting. "Long as I have her, she's my ticket to Mexico. Ain't no posse going to shoot indiscriminately at an outlaw who has a girl as his hostage."

Rushing's voice was even softer. "How will they know you've kidnapped her?"

"You're going to tell 'em, aren't you? 'Specially if it means the life of your child."

The farmer hesitated, then nodded.

Booe made an up-and-down movement with his Peacemaker. "If I can ask a favor of you, Mr. Rushing, face the other way and go kneel against the inside of them doors at the front of your barn. Close your eyes and count to 100. Complete that task and you are free to do as you wish. Bear with me for a week or so and I'll return your child and your horse, both untainted."

George Rushing turned slowly and moved toward the large front door of the barn, taking deliberate steps. Booe holstered his gun and nodded toward the back door. Callie pulled the reins of the filly and led her into the brilliant sunshine. A wave of weakness washed through him just as Booe managed to pull himself into the saddle. He headed Jack toward the concealing safety of the woods.

When they had ridden a quarter mile along the creek, Callie turned to him and spoke. "Mexico? We're going to Mexico?"

"Oh hell no, Smelly. And any legitimate lawman would know that was a subterfuge. But it will confuse the locals and make them wait another hour or two deciding which way to ride. That, plus the hour it will take Rushing to get the word out, and we'll be substantially on our way to the Red River."

She smiled at him, a sweet pretty smile.

Chapter 5
Hunt for a White Mule

There was scant conversation between Booe and the girl during their first day traveling toward the Kiamichi Boys encampment. The silence was in part because the misery of his wounds and the way in which the weakness perpetrated by his increasing fever forced him to concentrate completely on moving forward. And in part because he knew it was still possible for lawmen and posses to be lurking along their way. When they forded the Red River into the Indian Nations not long before dusk, he had a great sense of relief and release. Still, he feared, there might be rogue bounty hunters who would cross the river in hopes of killing him and taking his body back to Texas. There were as well bushwhackers and robbers who would not hesitate to kill him to get their hands on the money he had stolen from the bank in Bonham. If they killed him, he knew, they would have their way with the girl and then kill her. He was intent on surviving the trip successfully not only for himself, but to bring her to safety.

They made camp in a concealed hollow that night. He was too weary to do more than unsaddle his pony and make a pallet for himself to sleep upon. Callie, however, found clear water and produced food she had packed. It had not been dark for more than an hour before he slept. When he went to sleep and when he woke, the girl was watching him.

The following morning his pain had diminished, but his awareness was compromised by the growing fever, it required supreme effort for him to pull himself into the saddle. He decided to ride behind the girl, his head drooping occasionally and dizziness coming upon him once and again. Booe told the girl what landmarks to watch for and what danger signs she might encounter. The route they were taking was not the most traveled path and would require several more hours for the transit, but was less known and less exposed.

At length he realized he needed something to keep him focused so that he did not fall off his pony. He nudged Jack forward and caught up with the girl, who glanced over her shoulder at him. The trail was wide enough for two and they rode side by side.

"Talk to me, Callie."

"Very well. . . . Any particular subject you wish to discuss, Richmond Booe?"

He chuckled. "Well, for starters, you mind me asking why you always call me by both names? Richmond Booe? Do you know another feller named Richmond and you're just trying to keep us straight in your head?"

"Nope." She pursed her lips. "I suppose I don't know you well enough and I'm not impolite enough—despite contrary opinion—to call you simply by your first name. On the other hand, unlike my uncle, I cannot humble myself to the point of calling you 'Mr. Booe.'"

"I see. Well . . . call me what you will. Does it offend you for me to call you 'Callie?'"

"No."

"Callie what? What is your last name?"

"Dunlap."

"Dunlap?" He straightened in the saddle, turning toward her. "I gunned a fellow in Sherman a couple years ago name of Dunlap. He's not—"

"No. No kin. Though I must say my father did die of a single gunshot wound. He was in a card game in a town called Mesquite about seven years ago. . . . Isn't it odd the way so many men die by virtue of firearms? Seems to be a natural hazard in Texas. Tornadoes, rattlesnakes and gunpowder."

He shook his head. "Well, more die of hot lead than twisters or snakes put together. You don't have to be a bank robber to get shot round these parts. But . . . what about your mom. I take it she's not living either?"

"No. She died about nine or ten months after Papa. I was, I guess, ten-years-old when Momma died."

He waited for her to continue and, when she did not, he asked, "If I may inquire, what was the cause of your mother's passing?"

"Well . . ." She stared straight down the trail before them. "My aunt is fond of saying that Momma never recovered from my father's sudden death. She says she simply pined away for want of the one man she ever loved."

". . . You sound a little skeptical."

"At the time I thought that was about the stupidest thing I ever heard. I was more inclined to think it had something to do with the terrible flu that ran through the countryside that winter. I was sick and nearly died myself. I personally knew maybe two or three others who died with it. And I figured they couldn't all be pining away for want of tragic love."

Booe laughed and immediately caught his saddle horn to steady himself. "Whew. Well, so much for sweet love, I reckon. . . . Tell me about yourself, sis. What do you like doing? Are you still smoking grapevine?"

"No." There was disgust in her voice. "That was as unrewarding as it was difficult. I never saw any benefit to that. And I burned a hole in a dress trying to light up a vine. Didn't take long to decide never to try that again."

"Well, what do you like then?"

Callie searched the terrain on either side of the path, as if seeking an answer to his question. "I like fooling folks, Richmond Booe. I like it that nobody around really has any idea of what I'm really like."

He gazed at her curiously. "Why is that, exactly?"

"I'm not sure, exactly. Never have felt like I belonged on Uncle's farm. Sure have no inclination to live the way most girls my age end up living around there."

"Well . . . if you could do anything you wanted to do, what would it be?"

Her expression was wistful. "I think I'd like to go places.

67

I'd like to see the ocean. I'd like to learn things in museums and libraries and colleges." She glanced at him. "This is a learning trip for me, Richmond Booe. Being kidnapped by a famous outlaw is a once-in-a-lifetime occasion."

He grimaced. "Well, I hope it is. And let's hope it works out so that you can tell your grandkids all about it. Speaking of traveling, though, what with the money I'm setting aside for you, you ought to be able to go to all them places you were describing. Fancy museums and high-class libraries in great cities."

Callie shook her head. "Oh yes. I can see myself going to all those places. All alone. But I have some questions too, Richmond Booe. I want to know some things about you."

"Me."

"Yes, you."

"Ha. I don't know what there is to tell that ain't apparent. I'm well known. Notorious, if truth be told. All I had to do was ride down the main street of Bonham and in five minutes they had a welcoming party for me like nothing I've ever seen."

"What I want to know," she said, "is how you first got to robbing banks."

"Oh. That was easy enough. I just walked into a bank, pointed my pistol at the teller feller and said, 'Give me the money.'"

"Don't be coy, Richmond Booe. You know what I mean. Why did you start robbing banks in the first place?"

He studied her face, the fair, soft lines that he had to struggle to see in the darkness of the barn now distinct and pleasing in the clear late summer light. "Why would anybody care about that, Callie? Like you said yesterday morning, my place in perdition has long since been reserved. What does it matter why I started?"

She, who had confounded him regularly with expressions and verbiage he did not understand, gave him another odd look and then said, "When I am an old lady and I tell my grandchildren about being kidnapped by the infamous bank robber Richmond Booe, they will want to know what we talked about and what I asked you and why you robbed banks. So you see, this is not so much for me as it is those who will one day call me 'Granny.'"

He laughed and had to steady himself. "It's a pity I won't have the privilege of defending myself with those young'uns of yours, little sister. No telling what you're going to say about me."

She watched him, waiting for the explanation. He shrugged.

"Well, it was a bit of misfortune on my part," he said. "I had not intended to become a bank robber." He cleared his throat, deciding how to tell his story. "My mom was widowed in the war. It come to her that life in Texas held more promise than the struggling life we had in Mississippi. When we arrived in Texas, my ma had a fair bit of money from selling our old homestead. It was enough to buy some bottom land where we could build a house. Now she kept the bill of sale for the property in the bank in Silman, closest town to where the property was. Because she was a widow lady, she had to have a grown, male executor for the proper documents. But when the house finally got built and she set about having the deed registered, the scoundrel of a banker tried to pull a fast one. He said he couldn't sign the deed and execute it because Ma couldn't produce her deceased husband's birth certificate. It was clear his intent was to steal our property. And he had waited until the house was finished so it would be worth more."

As she listened, the girl watched him closely. Booe wondered why she was so focused on his story.

"Ma was all upset about it. My older brother, Tory—he's the oldest living brother, the two eldest died in the war along with Pap—said we needed to hire a lawyer because no judge would allow that rascal to get away with stealing the farm of a war widow. And then, there was me and my idea. I reckon I didn't have the patience or the trust to pay some lawyer to get justice for us. So I stepped up and did something." He glanced at her. "That was my way. I always been the one to take action. I always been the big and ugly one. Head and shoulders above everybody else and not willing to sit still for wrong doing from the time I was born, I reckon."

They rode in silence for a minute as he rested. At length he took a breath and continued.

"I got our horse and went into town to the bank. I walked right up to the banker, Horace Howard. He give me a look such like as I was of no account and says, 'What do you want, boy?' I expect he didn't have much of an opinion of me because I was all of sixteen." He turned to her. "Same age as you. I says to him, 'Mr. Howard, you are going to sign and seal that deed and give it to me right now.' He chuckles. Thought it was funny as hell. 'And if I choose not to do so?' he asks. So straightaway I slipped my Dragoon out of my coat and brought it smartly across the side of his head."

"Your what?"

Booe felt inside the saddlebag to his right and produced the massive pistol. "Colt's Dragoon." He held it out to her and, in taking it—startled at the weight—she almost dropped it. "Careful, sis. That's a helluva revolver. Single shot, .44 caliber cap-and-ball. It was the about the only thing of my daddy's that come home after the war. When I hit that banker with it, it opened his head right up. He fell out of his chair onto the floor. When he looked up, I pulled back the hammer and said, 'Mr. Howard, I got five rounds in this gun. I'm going to put them into you one-by-one. But, to make sure to retain your full attention, I'll be certain it's the last one that kills you. Now sign that deed, mister.'"

She watched him, waiting for him to continue. "Would you have shot him, unarmed and all?"

Booe considered it. "I don't know, Callie. I sure enough had a rage in me back then. But whether I would have killed him, the banker sure thought I would."

"So he signed the deed?"

"Yep. He had a change of heart right then in that moment. In fact he was right prompt in filling it out and signing it. He addressed it to the place down in Austin where they register deeds and sealed it with wax." Booe shook his head. "His hand was a shaking as he gave it to me. . . . I must say, that was the one minute in my life where I felt right, where I knew that justice had been served."

"So something must've gone wrong after that," the girl said.

He shrugged. "That was one proud man I had just humiliated and I reckon he was going to have the last word. So he says, 'Richmond Booe, you holding me at gunpoint inside a bank is the same as holding up the bank. You're going to the penitentiary. Well . . . I thought about it just that long. And sitting there was a leather mail pouch. I dumped everything out of it and turned around to the teller in the cage with the cash drawer. Scrawny little feller, he had been just a standing there watching all this, transfixed. And I says, 'Fill that up with all the money you got in your drawer, mister.' And of course he did as he was told.

"Then I went over to the banker and reached down inside his jacket and took his money pouch. Startled him, I'll tell you. And he says, 'Booe, I'll see you hang.' And I says, 'Whether I die before you or I die after you, Mr. Howard, you can be sure I'll meet up with you in hell and we will continue where we've left off.' And then I rode off. I went to Longview. I mailed the deed to Austin, robbed the bank in Longview and escaped across the Red River into the Indian Nations." He glanced at her. "I guess I been an outlaw ever since." He reflected on his encounter with the banker. "Odd thing is, I held that man up in his bank twice. The second time I was there to stop him from a new trick. He was trying to steal the land of my half-brother Jeremiah. Strange, isn't it, that I held up a banker twice to stop him from taking what wasn't his."

71

"That was sort of ironic, wasn't it?"

"Ironic? What's that mean?"

"Well," she said, "he was accusing you of being a thief when in fact he was the one about stealing your family's property."

He considered her words. "Well, Callie, some robbers wear high dollar suits and walk down the street without a worry in the word. And others of us sneak in the back way wherever we're going, living in fear of the noose and the six gun."

"What about prison? Aren't you afraid of going to jail?"

He laughed. "As it was explained to me, sis, if you commit a serious crime and somebody gets kilt, whether it was in self-defense or not, that makes you a murderer. I've known for a long, long time that my stay in any jail would last about as long as it took to build the gallows."

The girl shivered. She wrinkled her nose, as if speculating. "Have you ever thought of giving it up? Couldn't you quit taking the risk and just live somewhere you aren't wanted? I mean, based on your list you entrusted to me, all the land and all the money you have ought to be enough, don't you think?"

"Well surely to goodness." His voice was cavalier. "Truth is, I expect I will retire soon enough. We all do—all us desperados. Have you ever heard of an old bank robber?"

"No. I have not." She shook her head. There was something about the set of her jaw, fine and fair as it was, that suggested to him she did not want to discuss the topic further. "One thing, Richmond Booe."

"Yeah?"

"You are big, but you are not necessarily ugly."

He gazed at her. What did that mean? Was she saying he made himself ugly when he didn't need to be? Was his appearance ugly only to some folks and not others? What did she mean?

"By god, there is plenty times I really have no

72

understanding of what you mean when you say something."

She smiled.

"But I got a question for you, miss. You said, you thought it was foolish to think your mom pined away to death out of love for you father. You said, that's the way you felt at first. What do you mean by that? You mean you don't think that no longer?"

Callie took a breath, staring down the path before them. "Well. Love is not a thinking thing, Richmond Booe. It's a heart thing. Love makes people stupid and I guess we can all be stupid from time to time if the right individual happens along."

He considered her words. "Damn. I have no idea what you're saying."

"I'm saying you're white as a bleached sheet. Let's stop and eat something and rest."

Booe had not much appetite and the time of rest did little to restore his strength. When the sun began to set, he relied on the girl to find a concealed place to camp.

Though it was not cold, a chill came over him after dark. Even beneath the blanket and fully clothed, he shivered. The girl seemed to sense his condition and got beneath the blanket and pressed herself against his back, her arm around his shoulder and her hand on his. Comfort descended upon him quickly then and he slept.

The morning of the third day of the trip found him scarcely able to see at any distance. Like an inebriated man, he could only focus his eyes a few feet before him and, while he was able to stand, he could not walk in a distinct line.

Aware of his inability, the girl took to telling him what to do. She broke camp by herself and saddled both ponies. Gradually she coaxed him into stirrups and onto the back of his horse.

She spoke little as they rode and when she did it was mostly to encourage him. Even in his disoriented state, Booe knew she had been right. Had he attempted this trip by himself, he would never have completed it.

"By my estimate, Richmond Booe, we have only twelve or ten miles to Idabel. We should be there in time for lunch."

"You buying?" he mumbled.

He gazed at Jack's familiar, bobbing mane and found respite in the comfortable rocking motion. And then, before too long, they stopped for some reason that was unaccountable to him.

Booe raised his eyes and, for a brief instant, was able to see the great open door of a livery stable before him, faded black letters painted on the dull yellow: "Idabel Stable and Blacksmith." The girl had dismounted and was walking toward the dark interior as a man, pitchfork in his hands, emerged from the darkness. He was an Indian, extremely tall and powerfully built.

Booe heard the girl's voice. "We're on the hunt for a white mule. We heard tell you might have one here."

If the Indian looked down at the girl, it was only for an instant. Instead he was focused on Booe. He dropped the pitchfork and walked—unspeaking, showing no emotion— toward Booe. With no hesitation, he came to the side of the pony, reached out and pulled Booe into his arm. He slung him over his massive shoulder with no effort and walked toward the interior of the livery.

His voice was soft and clipped as he spoke to the girl. "Bring the horses. Tie them to back of the wagon."

No more was said.

Booe felt himself being lowered onto a bed of hay. He was, he realized, in the back of a wagon, stretched out on a very pleasant surface. In a moment he felt the girl settle beside him, sitting in the hay. His eyes closed, Booe drifted to unconsciousness.

Awareness came to him suddenly. Booe lurched, the straightening of his body revealing a single point of sharp pain, low in his back. He was lying in an actual bed on a real mattress. His fever was gone and he felt great fatigue, thirst and hunger.

In the moment he smelled rich tobacco smoke, he realized someone was sitting in a chair across the small room from his bed. It was a fellow in his fifties or early sixties, a thin, gray-haired man with a pipe resting in the side of his mouth.

The stranger slipped the piped from between his jaw teeth and spoke. "You lived."

His voice gravelly, Booe responded. "Seems I did."

"Credit to the young lady who brought you. And to Clear Water."

"Clear Water?"

He nodded. "She's the Indian woman who took the slug out of your back and used a poultice to draw out the poison."

Booe nodded. "A woman doctor. Second one."

"You would be Richmond Booe, would you not?"

"Yes, sir."

"And would your daddy have been Forrest Booe, a captain with the Mississippi Regulars in the war?"

He considered the man with new interest. "Yes, he was."

"I served with Captain Booe for the last eighteen months of his life. Was with him at Chickamauga at the time of his unfortunate passing. My name is Cullen Bartholomew."

Booe stared at the man, a strange feeling gathering in his chest. "Hello, Mr. Bartholomew. It is a pleasure, sir."

Bartholomew nodded and, sticking the pipe back in his mouth, spoke around the stem. "One hell of an officer was your father. Brave and smart in the thick of battle."

For an instant, Booe wondered if his own steadfastness in the face of gunfire had been handed down to him in some uncanny way by this father.

"I was only five when Pap and my two brothers rode off to war, Mr. Bartholomew. Often I wondered what it was like with them. In particular, how they died."

"About your brothers, I am unaware. They both perished before your father. I do know of his unfortunate

75

circumstances however. Union artillery, Mr. Booe. A ten pounder landed not a dozen feet from your daddy and he was gone in an instant. No suffering a-tall."

Booe considered his words. "There is some comfort in that. I take it he was staunch for the cause?"

"Oh hell no." Bartholomew shook his head. "Towards the end he was very quiet and kept predominantly to hisself. On the one occasion he spoke—through the liberal use of some corn liquor—he offered up to me personally that the war had cost him two sons and, if the North won and freed the slaves, it would cost him another."

Booe felt his jaw drop open. He had no idea that his father, Forrest Booe, considered Jeremiah—the son of his slave Bessie—a cherished son. Grief overcame him and his face, pointed downward toward the bed, showed the nearness of weeping.

Bartholomew got to his feet and stepped to the door. "I did not mean to upset you, sir. I meant only to convey the thanks to you that I never got to express to your father."

"Thank you, Cullen. May I call you Cullen?"

"Honored if you would."

"Thank you. I hope we get to speak again, soon."

He opened the door and stood with his hand on the knob, his face illuminated by the clear sunlight outside. "I'll tell the young lady you're awake. She's been asking after you."

Bartholomew disappeared, the door shutting quietly. Booe raised his head after a time and gazed about the room. His last prior memory was of the livery stable in Idabel. He assumed he was at the camp of the Kiamichi Boys in the Ouachita Mountains. Beyond that he felt relief and fatigue. Where was the girl?

That question was answered within a minute when the door opened again and Callie entered. She carried a tray of food and drink, but what most captured his attention was the brightly colored dress she wore—a pattern of sunny yellow and light blue. He smiled, relieved again that the girl was safe.

"You survived once more, Richmond Booe," she said, setting the tray on the table beside his bed. She stood looking at him, hands on her hips. "That's the most color I've seen in your face since the very first time I saw you."

"It's my pleasure to oblige, Miss Callie Dunlap. And speaking of color, that is a most attractive outfit your wearing. I'm curious as to why you seem to have abandoned your preference for dowdy shades of faded muslin."

She tried to hold back a smile. Apparently, Booe realized, she was glad he had noticed her nice dress.

"Clear Water is a doctor."

He nodded. "That'd be the Indian woman who took the slug out of my back."

"Yes. And Clear Water's daughter, Constance, is a seamstress." She held out her arms and stepped back from the bed. "Isn't it lovely. This may be the first new dress I've had since my mother died."

"She sowed it overnight?"

Callie's head dropped to one side. "She sewed it over two nights. . . . Richmond Booe, you've been sleeping for more than two days." She stepped back to the little table beside the bed. "Which is why I came to see you. You need to drink and to eat." She picked up a tiny, folded packet of paper, unfolded it and from it poured powder into a glass of water on the tray. "Clear Water says to drink this first."

"What is it?"

She stirred the mixture with a spoon. "Laudanum if I don't miss my guess."

"Painkiller. What makes her think I'm in pain?"

"She says you'd be trying to get up and move about after you woke up. She said you wouldn't know how much you were hurting until then." Callie handed him the glass.

"Well." He gazed from the liquid to the girl. "Reckon I better do what the doctor tells me. Especially what with her saving my life."

Booe scooted backwards so he could sit up in the bed.

Indeed, the pain in his back was sharp. The elixir was exceedingly bitter, but his thirst overcame the flavor and he downed the water swiftly. The girl placed the plate of food in his lap and sat down on the foot of the bed to watch him eat.

"This be meatloaf if I'm not mistaken."

"Yes," she replied. "With brown gravy. Those tomatoes were pulled fresh this morning, along with the fried okra. And the cornbread is just out of the oven."

The meatloaf seemed to Booe to be the most wonderful bite of food he had ever tasted. "Oh lord . . . this is some special feast, little sister."

"They eat like this around here all the time," she said. "Constance told me."

Booe stared at her. This time the underlying meaning of her words was more apparent to him.

"You fancy staying here, do you?"

She leaned toward him, eagerness on her face. "I think Clear Water could teach me a lot about doctoring. And I could learn to sew and get mail order books to read. There's a train station, I'm told, about forty miles from here. We could explore the whole world."

"We?" He frowned. "You got me figured into this?"

She leaned back, startled. "I—I mean . . . this is that place I was describing to you, Richmond Booe. No one who doesn't belong even knows where this place is. This is where you retire and live from the money you already have."

He gazed at her face—gentle, lovely, beguiling—for a long time before he spoke. "Callie, I don't mean to disappoint you, but the money I have cannot support this whole camp. And these fellers here, they won't stand by to be took care of. . . . As far as doctoring goes, being that these gents, same as me, rob banks for a living, you'd get lots of practice sewing up bullet holes. That's for sure." He swallowed. "The main thing, though, is I give my word."

"Gave your word?"

"To your uncle."

"What word?"

"I promised him I would bring back that painted pony. And you with it. Both unharmed."

And now it was the girl who sat in silence staring at him. It seemed to Booe that her face darkened, though her expression did not change. She stood up slowly.

"What craziness is this?" she said, looking about the room as if searching for something. "Rich, important men think nothing of breaking their word while desperate, hunted outlaws always keep theirs? I do not understand."

She turned her gaze upon him, as if suddenly aware of his presence. Leaning across the bed, she extended both hands and grabbed his hair behind his ears so that his head was immobile. Then she kissed him, a hard, long, longing kiss that thrilled and stunned him. Then, just as quickly, she pushed his head backwards and rose and took two steps toward the door before she stopped and looked back over her shoulder at him, her face full of fury.

"I hate you, Richmond Booe! I hate you! I hate you!"

He stared at her, stunned. "What one hell of a strange way you have of showing it."

She was at the door then, pulling it open and in the same instant the figure of Cotton Neal filled it. He had to turn sideways to allow the girl to storm out. Neal watched her run away, then stepped into the room and closed the door.

"Howdy."

"Hello, Cotton. Good to see you."

Neal came to the bed and Booe leaned forward, wincing, his hand outstretched.

"Keep your seat. Keep your seat," Neal said, shaking his hand.

"I owe you more than I can ever repay, friend."

"We were pleased to be of service, Richmond. You were gravelly in need of assistance."

"I was. And it will be my first order of duty when I leave this room to find Miss Clear Water to express my gratitude for saving my life."

Neal nodded. "Miss Clear Water is in truth Mrs. Cotton Neal."

"Oh. I see. And that makes Constance your daughter?"

"Correct."

Booe gazed at Neal. "It's none of my business, I know, but I got a particular reason for asking you a certain question."

"What's that?"

"How does it sit with your wife and daughter, you being in this sort of dangerous occupation of ours?"

"Bothers her, I reckon." Neal eased into the ladderback chair where Bartholomew sat before. "To her credit, she says nothing of it." He leaned back. "Why do you ask?"

"That girl who flung you aside as she departed. She is greatly taken with the life you all live here in the mountains. Her desire is to remain here."

"And she left in a rage because you won't let her?"

Booe sighed in exasperation. "It's not up to me where she lives on down the road. First, unfortunately, I have to return her to her uncle's farm, along with that filly she rides. I give my word that I would return the horse and the girl unscathed."

"I see," Neal said thoughtfully. "And you're bound to keep that promise?"

"Cotton, if I don't die in a hail of lead, I will most certainly die on the gallows. I rob banks. I shoot people who are trying to shoot me. I do not want to die for horse thieving or kidnapping some half-grown maiden girl."

"I see." Neal ran his hand through the thinning hair atop his head. "She's marrying age, you know."

"She's just a kid."

"She's got a suitor—besides you."

Booe's head tilted to one side. "Do tell."

"Yep. Boy name of Tom Franklin."

"He in your gang?"

"Well, kinda. Tom is an orphan. His momma died when he was born and his dad, a few years ago, had a fatal encounter with a noose over in Durango. We sort of took Tom in and raised him. He's about fourteen or so." Neal shook his head, grinning. "He sure took a shine to Miss Callie. Follows her around like a moth follers a candle."

Booe's eyebrows arched. "And she feels the same about him?"

"Oh lord no. I don't think she knows he exists. The girl loves you, Richmond."

He caught his breath and felt a quick sting in his back. "Callie is too smart to be in love with me." The instant he spoke Booe remembered her words, that love can make anyone stupid.

"I don't know how stupid she is. Seems pretty smart to me. But the one thing I do know is that she has no one but you in her heart, Richmond."

Booe dropped his chin and rubbed his forehead with his hand. "I don't understand that girl at all. She says things that I cannot apprehend even after studying on them."

"I took you for a man of the world, Richmond. Hard to imagine a fellow like you getting buffaloed by some young farm girl. Unless you had some feeling for her too."

Booe glanced at Neal as if he had said something outrageous.

"Well, at any rate," Neal said, "I come to check up on your condition. That, and to ask if you're interested in riding with us on a job later this week—should you be able."

He took a breath. Armed robbery seemed a safer subject than sweet love.

"A bank job, I take it?"

"Yes," Neal said. "Not too awful far from where you were last. There's a company bank in a place called Clarksville."

"I know that town."

"Well there's a horse drawn millworks in that town that

81

gins cotton and turns it into cloth. They have about eighty workers, all of whom line up to get paid on Fridays."

"Yeah?"

"I've been sending a couple of my boys—unknown to locals so far as I know—to check out the payroll routine of the bank. First Friday of each month, a disbursement of cash comes in on a train. It's a month's worth of cash for all the workers at the factory, plus assorted other businesses and concerns in the town. Cash arrives mid-morning. Workers get paid late afternoon."

Booe pursed his lips. "Correct me if I'm wrong, but with a payout that large, won't there be additional armed guards?"

"We've planned for that. We'll have six fellers mounted and riding in, plus the boy Tom will be sitting outside of town with saddled horses and spare guns. Still, having somebody like you, who's known to remain calm while under fire, with us would be a great benefit."

Booe reflected silently on the prospects of robbing the Clarksville bank.

"The boys have drawn a diagram of the bank. We have our positions planned. We've figured out how long it should take and set the course for our best route back out of town and across the river."

"When do you leave and how long a ride will it be?"

"Day and a half. We leave first thing Thursday morning. Camp just this side of the river. Set out by dawn Friday. Puts us in Clarksville just about lunch time. The boys have timed it on three separate occasions."

Drawing a deep breath, this time without the pain of the last week, Booe pursed his lips. "Cotton, you all were going to rob this bank even before I showed up, weren't you?"

"We were, yes."

"Sounds to me like you have a well-figured plan with all contingencies accounted for. If I were to throw in with you, it wouldn't mean nothing to the boys except splitting it eight ways instead of seven."

Neal shrugged. "None of the boys would begrudge you that, Richmond." Suddenly he smiled broadly. "I don't think you understand the gravity your presence would lend to a job such as this."

"Gravity?"

He chuckled. "We heard about the shootout in Bonham, how bad it was. Frankly we weren't sure you got out of there in one piece. Yet here you are, purt near good as new. . . . You shot eight men, Richmond. Killed three. You're a legend. When people see you, it puts fear into 'em. Except our men. If you were to ride with us, it would put confidence in 'em."

". . . Cotton, I reckon it's bad of me to demur, especially owing you all my life as I do, but I think I'll sit this one out. However, I do like the idea of somebody having my back and I'm impressed by the extent of the planning you've done. With me, I've always relied on surprising folks. Sometimes the bank has plenty of money and sometimes it's destitute. It's feast or famine. Maybe I should change my way of operating. So after I take the girl back home—and after you all finish with Clarksville—maybe the best thing for me to do is join up with you. Assuming the invite is still open."

Neal got to his feet. "You are always welcome here and with the Kiamichi Boys, Richmond. In case you'd like the security of traveling with friends, you can ride along with us three days hence. If I don't miss in my estimation, Clarksville's not but a couple dozen miles from the farm where the girl lives."

He nodded. "I'll take you up on that, Cotton. Maybe if we all ride together the girl will be easier to get along with."

Chapter 6
Detour on the Way Home

Booe had wondered if Callie would protest or even, as she had when he demanded that she not accompany him to Idabel, simply refuse his directives. On Thursday morning, however, when he—still aching and moving slowly—made his way to barn where Jack was stabled, he found her waiting. She had already saddled Millie. The girl said nothing and Booe thought it wise not to try to provoke her by trying to start a conversation. Though there was little light in the hour just before daybreak, it seemed to him that she was near tears. When the procession of nine riders and six extra horses started down the mountain trail headed south, she rode near the back, while Booe rode at the front alongside Cotton Neal. Periodically, as casually as he could, Booe looked over his shoulder to see if she was still with the group.

The back trail they rode toward the Red River, though less traveled, was clear enough that they made their way without encountering obstruction or delay. When they stopped at midday to eat, they were, as intended, halfway to Texas.

Again in the afternoon, Booe rode at the head of the column with Neal. Cullen Bartholomew joined them for a time, and the three spoke their remembrances of the war years, of the reconstruction that followed and of the changes they had experienced. Booe was still trying to remember the names of the other men riding with them: the brothers Spencer and Jake Easterly, Warren Rives and Jonathan Poole. Riding at the back of the string was Tom Franklin and beside him was Callie. Each time Booe looked back it seemed that Tom was talking to her, while she said nothing, her face expressionless.

The Easterly brothers, Booe learned, having never been identified in the course of a robbery, were not wanted for any crime in Texas. Thus it could be assumed they had aroused no suspicion during their three prior trips to Clarksville. The information they provided, Neal assured Booe, had been accurate at every turn. Based on their estimation of the payroll needs of the mill and the cash requirements of the local businesses, Neal anticipated they would take in between $8000 and $9000. Despite the risk of additional guards being present, the men were ready to take their chances for a payoff of a $1000 each—or more.

As Booe listened to the details of the robbery plan again and again, he felt a growing wariness and a sense of relief that he had decided not to participate in this robbery. Perhaps, he told himself, it was simply an unwillingness to be shot at so soon after the wounds he had sustained in Bonham. And it crossed his mind that, if he were shot, this time he could not flee to Callie for help.

An hour before dark they came to the Red River. Quickly and silently they set up camp in the scrub oak timber and tall grass on the Indian Nations side. They ate provender that did not need to be cooked so they would have no visible campfire.

To Booe's surprise, the girl came to him just before dark. Wordlessly she spread her bedroll beside his and lay down, her back to him. Lying on his back, sensing her nearness, Booe remembered the trip north and how, when he was so feverish during the last night, she had gotten beneath the blanket with him and put her arm around him, her hand on his hand. He felt a deep and abiding sadness and fought against it by reminding himself of his pledge to return the filly and the girl unharmed.

Cullen Bartholomew woke him in the morning with a touch. He nodded toward the girl, indicating that Booe should wake her quietly. Everything was to be silent from this point. The rest of the trip to Clarksville was to be ridden in tree lines and creek beds so they might avoid being seen.

Booe felt a great reluctance to wake Callie, in part because he wanted her to be able to sleep. Of course by the late afternoon she would be home and could rest as much as her uncle and aunt would allow. His hesitation, he realized, was more because he sensed her unhappiness and knew he was the source of it. Why did it give him such pause to upset this farm girl? Perhaps it was the recognition that, within a day's time, she would forever be out of his life. And indeed he would miss her profoundly.

When he reached out gingerly for her shoulder, she turned onto her stomach away from his hand. At first he thought she had merely moved in her sleep. But when she sat up and stood and began to secure her bedroll, he realized she had been awake.

They mounted their horses as quietly as possible and forded the sandy, shallow stream. An abiding watchfulness descended on Booe. Now he was back in Texas and subject to being shot by any lawman or citizen, who would be rewarded handsomely for his demise.

When they made the first tree line south of the river and Booe was able to relax and take a deep breath, he realized the girl had been riding just behind him. He reined in his pony until she pulled alongside.

"Are you speaking to me today?" he asked, keeping his voice low.

She didn't look at him as she replied. "I don't know. Are you feverish, pale as a ghost, unable to raise your eyes and too weak to walk on your own?"

He chuckled. "I think I'm picking up on the meaning of the things you say more and more. So in case I haven't expressed my appreciation quite enough, allow me to thank you yet once again for the splendid way you saved my life. Truth be told, you saved it repeatedly."

He waited for her to respond. When she did not, he rode on beside her silently.

Ten minutes later, she began to speak. "What would you be doing, Richmond Booe, if you were not taking me back to Uncle's farm?"

"Me? . . . Reckon I'd be headed back to my own place up near Yukon. Either that or waiting in the camp up on the mountain for Cotton and the boys to get back from their excursion."

"You wouldn't be riding with them to help rob the bank in Clarksville?"

He faced her. "So you know where they're going, do you?"

"Tom told me. Tom wants to tell me everything. It got so I couldn't ride beside him because he talks constantly, mostly about things that hold no interest for me."

"Well, I reckon the boy's sweet on you, Callie."

"I'm an unattached female of breeding age. That's what he's attracted to."

When Booe laughed, she glanced in his direction and said, "So anyway, are you saying you wouldn't be riding along with these boys to rob this big bank that's full of payroll money?"

He drew a breath and shook his head. "Naw. Not really." He glanced back to make sure no one was close enough to hear their conversation. "I'm right impressed with how well they have planned this out, Callie, but this ain't my preferred way of robbing a bank."

"You rob by yourself, don't you? That way you only have to split the money with the lady who sews up your bullet wounds?"

He chuckled. "No. I don't mind sharing the proceeds, especially if I weren't the only one taking the risk. The problem is, the more you plan things out and the longer you take to pull off the job, the more things can change. You run the risk of losing the edge surprise gives you."

"Didn't help you much in Bonham."

". . . Well, you got me there. Of course, as much as them

87

boys prepared for a Richmond Booe sort of outlaw to ride into town, when I did come knocking, it shore didn't work out the way they planned either, now did it?"

She thought about his words. "So how are you going to keep from getting shot up in the future?"

"I'm not sure. Which is not to say I haven't been thinking about it. I have. I also been thinking about what you said."

She tilted her chin. "What did I say?"

"You said I should retire."

Her eyes widened. "You're going to retire?"

Booe shook his head. "Naw. I just thought about it. The way a feller who can't swim thinks of jumping into a fast-flowing river—then he changes his mind." When she turned away and did not laugh and did not reply, he asked, "You still hate me?"

Her jaw set primly, she said, "If I said I would hate you for the rest of your life, do you think that would be a long time?"

"Okay, answer me this: why do you hate me?"

She turned toward him. "I don't hate you, Richmond Booe."

He studied her face. "Why did you say you did?"

". . . Because hating and loving somebody are dresses cut from the same cloth."

Booe thought about her words. ". . . Hell and damnation. Are you saying you love me?"

"I'm not saying anything. I'm just trying to explain something to a man who is too stupid to understand what I'm trying to explain."

He rode for a minute staring at her. He didn't know how to respond.

Her mouth taut, Callie said, "Yes I love you. . . . You fool." When he continued to stare and did not speak in reply, she said, "Are you going to demean me for saying that? Are you going to say I'm just a kid, like you did before? . . . Are you going to tell me I'd be better off with someone like that idiot boy, Tom?"

"Oh god no!" Booe said abruptly. "Don't you see, Callie, he's no better off than me. Here in the next year or so, he's going to be the one riding in with a gun and holding up banks too. He's a young un, true. But still, he has no more of a future than I do." He shrugged. "Now, if maybe you could convince him to give up outlawing—"

"Why not you?"

"What?"

"If I can't convince you to give it up, what makes you think I could convince him?"

Riding with his head down, Booe reflected on what she had asked him. "Well, supposing that I gave up robbing banks and supposing I did it because you love me. Then what?"

She gave him a sort of look that implied he was missing something obvious. "Then I wouldn't have to sew you up anymore, or spend sleepless nights wondering if you're going to be alive when I wake up the next morning, or pine away wondering if I'll ever see you again."

"What?" He turned in the saddle. "I was with you until that last."

As he watched her, her face staring straight down the trail ahead of them, her cheeks slowly turned a ruddy red, made all the more obvious by the fairness of her skin and hair. She looked down, then spoke.

"You are taking me back to my prison. And probably soon enough you'll be in a bone orchard. . . . So I'm going to go ahead and say this. I won't have another chance. . . . When you came into my uncle's barn last year, Richmond Booe, that was the most exhilarating, terrifying moment of my life. It took me about thirty seconds to realize you weren't going to kill me. Or rape me. . . . And watching you move across the loft, looking out at the posse who came to take you in, that was so exciting I could not believe it was happening. I laid awake all that night. . . . And I said to myself, 'If ever Richmond Booe comes back to me, I will never let him go.' I could think of nothing but you." She shrugged. "Although I have no idea how I thought I was going to keep you if you ever did come back."

Unaccountably, her chin quivered and she started to weep, tears lining her crimson cheeks as she continued. "Then, a week ago, you did come back into my life. . . . When I saw Jack and found your saddle in the stall, I was excited beyond words. Then I found you all shot up in the loft, and I was horrified. I just wanted to disappear. I thought to myself, 'If he dies, I will die as well.' But you lived. Despite my best efforts. And you didn't learn the lesson all those bullets were trying to teach you. So now you're going back to robbing banks, knowing that everyone in Texas is on the hunt for you—especially after you shot all those men in Bonham. . . . What I want is the one thing I cannot have. You will not give up being a desperado. . . . That, and you won't keep me with you. . . . I just want to die."

He wanted immediately to tell her how wrong she was to care for him, that he had no future to share with such a fine, unique person. He wanted to speak of the admiration he felt for her, and the gratitude. He wanted to console her.

"Callie, I—"

"Ssh." She cut him off. "Ssh. Be quiet, Richmond Booe. Just for once be smart enough not to say a word. There is nothing you can say."

So he did not speak.

They rode together, their eyes on the trail before them and their thoughts on the conversation and on what was unfolding. He knew the girl was right. Yet he had never heard of an outlaw who gave up robbing banks just for the sake of a young girl's request. That and he had no idea how he could be part of her life even if he did stop being an outlaw. Booe did not know how to respond, either to the girl or to the strange feelings turning within him.

About the middle of the morning Cotton Neal pulled his horse alongside them. His voice low, he said, "Here in the next hour or so we'll be outside of Clarksville. You staying with us until then?"

Booe nodded. "We go right by there on the way to her uncle's farm. Do you need us to split up now?"

"No. We're coming in on the south side of town and there's a ridge that runs about a quarter mile outside of the center of Clarksville. It obscures any traveler from being seen by folks down in the town. The Easterly boys have this all mapped out."

"I reckon we'll stay with you until you ride into town then."

"When we stop there and you all head on, Tom will wait at the trailhead with the extra horses. Me and the boys will gallop down to the bank and stick it up. We figure we'll have the guards outnumbered, just in case they try to be heroes." He nodded at Booe. "If you don't mind me asking, what are your plans from here, Richmond?"

He smiled. "Well, after my safe-and-sound delivery, I intended to head back to your place in the mountains and talk over how things transpired for you. However, as I been studying on it, after you all hold up the payroll, this place is going to be a beehive of constabulary looking for you. So I think maybe I'll camp out in the woods for a night or two. Maybe take the long way around through Arkansas and come back over the east side of the mountain. So I figure I'll be back to your camp in four or five days."

"Yeah. That sounds like it would work substantially." Neal turned his gaze to the girl. "Miss Callie, we sure have enjoyed having you with us in the Kiamichis."

She gave him a tight smile. "I learned a lot, Mr. Neal. I thank you for your hospitality as well."

"Clear Water was quite taken with you. As was my daughter Constance."

"They are lovely people, Mr. Neal. I would have enjoyed getting to know them more."

Neal hesitated, then decided not to address the issue of

whether or not Callie would ever be at the Idabel mountain camp again. "Well, we will all miss you. Tom most of all will miss you, I expect."

Slowly, earnestly, she nodded. "I so enjoyed my stay with you, Mr. Neal that, at this moment the thought of not having to listen to Tom ever again is my only real consolation."

Neal laughed aloud, then quickly covered his mouth and looked around himself. "Here I tell everybody to keep it down, then I bust out." He tightened his grip on his reins and, just before he spurred his horse to go back to the head of the column, he said, "I reckon we'll stop momentarily at the trailhead and say our goodbyes."

Callie rode beside him wordlessly for the next hour, her countenance trained forward, but down. Booe could feel the growing seriousness of the column of riders around him—the same fearful excitement that gripped him in the uncertain hour just before each job he pulled.

They emerged from a stand of live oak and scrub cedars into a clearing where there was a large earthen berm to his left and a wooded area to his right. A couple hundred yards from the tree line was a worn path that led over the berm. Two riders, the Easterly brothers, whipped past them and stopped at the trailhead. They were joined by Cotton Neal and Cullen Bartholomew. Booe and Callie stopped beside them as they waited for Jonathan Poole and Warren Rives. Tom Franklin came up to the group riding slowly so the half dozen horses he led would remain quiet.

"Everybody loaded and ready?" Neal's voice was low. "Everybody know what to expect?" He looked to Booe. "Thanks for riding with us. Any advice you have for us?"

"Naw. You all know what you're doing better than me. If you boys should fall into large sums of money, try not to spend it all in one place. Put a little in the bank."

There was a soft chuckling from the men.

"Actually that's what I'm looking for, Richmond," Jacob

Easterly said. "I been hunting for a bank that can't be robbed. Ain't found one yet."

"Well, keep your heads down," Booe replied. "If I get two or three miles down the trail here and I don't hear no shooting, I'll know everything came off like you planned."

"Let's go," Neal barked.

Instantly the half dozen bank robbers spurred their ponies and rode over the ridge and disappeared. The troop of spare horses danced about and calmed as Tom held their reins and watched after the riders.

He looked toward the girl. "Sure good to meet you, Miss Callie."

"Likewise, Tom."

His eyebrows arched in an expression of confident bravado. "If you should ever come back to mountain camp, I'd be pleased to put aside any bank robbing I was about to do and visit with you about—uh, whatever you'd like."

"I'm sure that's true, Tom," she said. "I cannot think of anything that makes me feel more dubious." She urged Millie forward.

Booe fell in beside her, glancing back to see when they were out of Tom's hearing range.

"He has no idea you were making fun of him."

"Wouldn't matter if he did."

They had not quite made it to the tree line at the far side of the clearing when they heard the report of a rifle, followed immediately by a salvo of gunfire. Booe wheeled Jack back toward the berm. More shots—pistol and rifle fire—rang out.

"It's an ambush." He looked back to the girl. "Twenty or twenty-five miles Follow the path. When you get to—"

"I know where I am," she interrupted.

At the sound of more gunfire, he turned back toward the town.

"Richmond!"

He looked back to her. There was a second of reluctance he felt. It was the first time she had called him "Richmond."

93

He filled his lungs with air. "If I survive, I'll come back for you." Booe did not wait for her response. "Ha!"

Jack leaped forward as if he too understood where they were riding. Booe crested the hill to find Tom. The boy had ridden up over top of the berm and was looking down into the three dozen frame buildings that were the heart of Clarksville.

"There are gunmen across the street! The boys can't get into the front of the bank. They're pinned down behind a water trough."

"Follow behind me, Tom." Booe started down the hill toward the center of town. "Behind me on my left. I'm going to ride up on the lawmen from the side and blast away. When I do, you take the horses over to Cotton and the boys."

At full gallop, Booe reflexively tapped the stock of each of his pistols. Ahead of him he could see the bank to his left. Three horses—horses the Kiamichi boys had ridden in on—lay dead in front of the bank. Another, twenty yards further down the road, lay on its side, thrashing in its death throes.

"They pinned them down and shot their horses so they couldn't get away," Booe said to himself.

He galloped along the side of the road opposite the bank, out of the sight line of the gunmen, who were still firing at the water trough directly in front of the bank's door. As he drew closer to the battle, Booe could see a body—Jonathan Poole—lying lifeless in the street. Even at the distance, Booe could tell the man had been shot in the back. And there was another set of legs—he could not tell whose they were—protruding, motionless, past the trough in plain sight, revealing a number of bullet wounds.

Booe filled his right hand with the Peacemaker from the left side of his gun belt and cocked a round into firing position. It was only when he was upon them that he realized the gunmen were in front of a general store. They had created a false front that looked exactly like the bottom portion of the store from across the street, and behind it they had stacked sandbags.

Appearing above them from their left, Booe fired at the man closest to him just as the others were turning toward him. Hit dead center in the chest, the man flew backwards against the outer wall of the store. As they stared at him, Booe fired above their heads, the rounds splintering the wooden wall, that was already pocked with holes from the gun battle. Panicked, they fell to the ground, dodging and covering their heads. And as he fired, he counted: seven men, plus the first he shot.

"Throw down your guns!" he shouted. "Throw 'em down or die now."

A couple of the men tossed their weapons down immediately. As Booe looked down the row of them, he saw at the very end the familiar face of Avery Tubbs, a boy he gone to school with when he first moved to Texas. And Avery saw and recognized him.

"Richmond?"

Booe fired the last round from his Colt and hit Tubbs exactly where he intended, in his right shoulder, which burst apart and the rifle he had been holding spun forward through the air.

"Bushwhacker!" He holstered the .45 and pulled another from his right hip. "Throw down your guns! All of them! Go through the mercantile and out the back. You have five seconds before I start shooting." As the men began to scurry backwards, he called, "Take these wounded with you, bastards, or I'll drop you right beside 'em."

As the last of the ambushers disappeared into the store, Booe turned to face the bank. Tom, still on his pony, was handing reins down to two, slow-moving men—Warren Rives and Jacob Easterly. Lagging behind was Cotton Neal, hit once or twice about the neck, who was trying to help Spencer Easterly to his feet. Booe spurred Jack across the street and slid out of his saddle.

His voice calm, he spoke to Neal. "Can everybody ride?"

"Jonathan is dead," Neal said. He glanced down to the

other form lying askew, the upper half concealed by the trough.

Booe looked down into the eyes of Cullen Bartholomew, who stared back at him.

"Hello, Mr. Booe."

"How are you doing, Cullen? Can I give you a hand up?"

"No." There was the slightest shaking of his head. "That first shot hit me square in the back. Ain't felt my legs since then. Just as well. Them boys been using me for target practice."

"We'll put you on a horse, Cullen."

"No, no." He closed his eyes. "I couldn't hold myself on. And mostly I'd slow you all down." He looked up at Booe again. "A fellow ought to be able to stand on his own two feet for his own hanging, don't you think?"

"That's my intention."

"May I trouble you for a favor, Mr. Booe?"

"Of course."

"I emptied my revolver shooting over the top of the horse trough here. I'm flat out of bullets. Could I borrow a pistol from you? Just briefly?"

Booe did his best to keep his face emotionless as he reached within the interior pocket of his duster and produced the derringer.

"This here's a .32 caliber cap-and-ball pistol," he said, leaning down and sliding it into Bartholomew's hand. "It's got a mighty short barrel and only two rounds. So you have to be sure of what you're aiming at."

"Oh, I'm right sure, Mr. Booe." The thin, older man smiled at him. "I'm thankful to you."

Booe nodded.

"When I see your daddy here directly, Mr. Booe. I'll tell him you were a fair hand and calm under fire. You'd a made one helluva soldier."

"If you see Pap before I do, you tell him I've provided for his family. For every last one of them."

"I will, sir."

"Now, if you'll excuse me, Cullen, I've got some banking to attend to."

"I'll wait to see you leave, sir."

The other men, except for Neal, had mounted up. All were watching him.

"Can they all ride?" Booe asked Neal.

"Yeah. I expect so." Neal looked haggard.

Booe turned to the boy. "Tom, you know the way we came into town?"

"Yes, sir."

"Lead these men back out that same way. Unless one of them falls off a horse, you keep going until you cross the river. Understand?"

"Aren't you and Mr. Neal coming?"

"We will catch up with you before you get there. If we can." He waved his hand and startled the boy's horse. "Go now!"

And with that motion the four riders rode back up the trail toward the berm.

"What happened to the bushwhackers?"

"I disarmed 'em all and chased 'em into the mercantile. But I do not believe for a moment they aren't finding more firearms and headed back this way." He nodded toward the bank. "Did you not get in?"

"We tried, god knows, but they had it secured from the inside. You're not still thinking about getting to the money, are you?"

"You want the death of your men to amount to something, don't you?"

"Well yeah, but—"

Booe stepped to one of the dead horses in the street and pulled a double barrel shotgun from a scabbard. He pulled back both hammers and aimed at the center of the bank's wooden doors.

"Watch yourself."

The blast caused the doors to buckle and come loose from their bottom hinges, swinging freely. The wooden beam that had braced the inside had been splintered and dangled uselessly before the doors.

"Give me 90 seconds, Cotton. If I'm not back, ride on."

Neal spun the cylinder of his reloaded revolver. "I reckon I'll wait for you. As long as it takes. There may be armed men in there, you know."

He nodded. "I'll be right back."

Booe pulled the Dragoon from the back of his belt along with his spare Peacemaker. Pistols in either hand, he kicked one loose door from its hinges and stepped into the darkness of the bank. He stood listening as his eyes acclimated to the darkness. There was the slightest noise of something scooting across the wooden floor. Booe stepped toward the cashier's counter at the back of the room. Splintered wood and disarray were everywhere. The hail of bullets from the gunmen had left mayhem in the bank they were supposed to be protecting. When he rounded the counter, he saw an iron safe and a shivering man—dressed in the white shirt and black gartered sleeves of a teller—hiding behind it. Booe looked cautiously around the area.

"You the teller?"

"Yes, sir."

Booe wagged a gun at the safe. "The payroll money all in that safe?"

"Yes, sir."

"Well open it, son."

"No, no." The man shook his head. "It's not locked." He took hold of the handle, pulled it down and the door swung open soundlessly.

Booe motioned with his head and the man scooted out of the way.

"Hands where I can see 'em." He holstered the Colt, knelt in front of the open door and began scooping the banded stacks of money into the large, outer pockets of his duster. "Got a couple questions for you."

"Yes, sir."

"How did them boys know we was coming?"

The teller swallowed. "Easterly brothers. We figured out weeks ago who they were. Strangers asking questions about payroll delivery just stirs up suspicion."

"All right. One more. How much is the weekly payroll for the mill workers?"

"Uh. Uh. About eighty fellows. Ten a week. Be $800."

"That's good pay. Well earned. All right. See this?" Booe held up five stacks of $200 each. "This is $1000. I expect to read in the paper that the Kiamichi Boys left this week's payroll here in the safe and it was give to the mill workers. If'n I don't read that, I'll be back, so you can to me explain why this didn't go to the fellers who earned it. Understand?"

He nodded.

Booe stood and looked down at the teller. "Now listen, don't get down on yourself about losing your water like that. You probably thought I was going to kill you—which I would have if you hadn't done exactly what I told you. They say a lot of brave men can't hold their bladder when they're standing on the gallows. That might happen to me. Who knows?"

He walked back out the door and spoke to Neal, who was staring across the street. "Any sight of them bushwhackers?"

"Not yet."

"We got to be going."

Neal pulled himself onto the back of the last fresh horse as Booe mounted Jack. He looked down at Cullen, who gazed back at him with as peaceful a look as Booe had ever seen.

"Better head on out, Mr. Booe."

"My best to you, Cullen. God bless you."

They were halfway to the top of the berm when they heard the report of the derringer.

The two men rode in silence for half an hour.

Periodically Booe would look over his shoulder. They stopped at a spring fed brook once to let the horses drink while they listened for the sound of riders.

As they rode on toward the Red River, Neal touched the wounds on his neck and ear. Booe watched him from the corner of his eye. He knew the man's pain and weariness would increase greatly as the immediacy of the gunfight waned.

"A couple things I should tell you, Cotton."

"What's that?"

"You all underestimated the money in the bank by more than a third. There was fourteen thousand in there. Then too, I left $1000 in the bank."

"You did? Why?"

"That's a week's pay for those mill boys. No reason they shouldn't get what they earned. Mill work is damn near dangerous as bank robbing."

"Well, that would be Jonathan's agreed share. You'll take Cullen's share. . . . I know he would want that. We wouldn't have come out with anything if it weren't for you, Richmond. Fact is, we'd all be dead or locked up waiting to die. . . . We're much obliged to you."

"No more than I am to you. Clear Water saved my life. You all gave me and Callie complete hospitality."

"Speaking of which, what became of the girl when the shooting started?"

"I sent her on down the trail. She said she knew the way and I reckon she did."

"You gonna check on her?"

Booe sighed and pushed his hat back on his head. "We better catch up with Tom and the others and see how they are. Once I get you all to Idabel and make sure you're on the way to mending—and once things settle down in these parts—I may ride on down just to see if Callie got home safe."

100

Chapter 7
Back to Church

It occurred to Booe, as he walked Jack into the clearing, past the little church, toward the hitching rails, that he was in a perfect disguise. No one who saw him—wearing a black suit and tie, leading a giant draft horse up to a church on Sunday morning—would think for an instant he was a notorious bank robber.

He saw Millie as he approached the row of horses and buggies. She was hitched to George Rushing's wagon. Booe casually tied the Percheron gelding beside her and unharnessed the little paint. He pulled the saddle off the giant horse and deftly slid it onto the smaller horse. Millie, who recognized him, turned back to watch him a time or two, more out of curiosity than concern.

"I'm glad to see you found your way home, Millie the filly. Now let's go see how little sister is fairing."

As he walked across the yard toward the front of the building, Booe saw a tow-headed boy—seven or eight-years-old—sitting cross-legged on the steps. He watched Booe without moving as he stopped in front of the church door.

"How you?" Booe asked.

"I'm good." The boy squinted up at him. "How you?"

"Twixt hay and stray." Booe tilted his head. "You know who I am?"

"Revival preacher?"

"Nope."

"Good." The child was obviously relieved. "Who are you then?"

"Bank robber."

"No you're not."

"How'd you know that?"

101

"No banks open on Sunday."

"Oh. Well I reckon I might as well go in and get some religion then." He pursed his lips. "Speaking of which, how is it you're out here instead of being in yonder singing and praying."

"Had to go to the outhouse."

"Well, I'm pretty new here, but I believe I saw the outhouse around back as I rode up."

"Already been."

"Um-hmm. And you ain't going back inside?"

"Most of 'em like it better when I stay outside. Specially the preacher. Says I squirm and chatter."

"I see. For some reason you remind me of someone I know. Well, as long as you're lingering, how'd you like to make some for-real money?"

The boy eyed him suspiciously. "Doing what?"

Booe nodded toward the cloistered animals. "Watching my horses. They're pretty valuable to me. If a rider or two was to come up, I'd appreciate it if you'd come in and tell me—just to be on the safe side."

"How much?"

"Would a dime get it?"

"A dime!" The boy stood up. "Sure thing, mister!"

Booe produced the coin and had it yanked away by the boy, who sat back down immediately and stared at the horses. Booe patted him on the head, stepped up to the wooden doors of the Calvary Baptist Church and opened them as quietly as he could.

There was an anteroom inside, so Booe could stand to one side without being seen by the preacher, whose forceful voice was the only sound from inside the sanctuary. Booe listened to him and watched him for a moment: a painfully thin, balding man who had pulled off his jacket and was sweating profusely as he yelled at the devil.

There was a three-level wooden shelf to the right side of the anteroom, the top shelf just higher than Booe's sight line.

He pulled another coin—larger, heavier and made of gold—from the pocket of his vest and slid it all the way back to where the shelf met the wall.

With that, he rested his right hand on the butt of the Peacemaker stuck in the left side of his belt and stepped into the back of the room, standing silently in the center aisle. The minister stopped preaching instantly. The congregation, four dozen souls, turned as one to the back of the nave to see what it took to silence their preacher. Booe could tell as they faced him that a good many recognized him. In the same instant, he saw Callie, sitting by herself on the very front pew—the mourner's bench. Once again wearing a maudlin, faded dress, she had been made to sit in the place of sinners, in the sight of all, to atone for whatever wrongs they assumed she had done. Booe tasted brass and took a full breath.

"Morning, folks," he said calmly. "My name is Richmond Booe." He swung the Colt into view, using the barrel to push the hat back on his head. "I need every one of you—man, woman and child—to reach out and put both your hands on the back of the pew in front of you and keep looking at the pastor up there."

Booe watched the congregation carefully as they obeyed him. One fellow in his early 30s hesitated, extending his hands only slowly and turning his head just slightly so he might be able to look backwards from the corner of his eye. Booe walked to him, midway up the center aisle, slowly but directly. The man caught his breath as Booe reached inside the fellow's dress jacket and produced the revolver.

"What possessed you to bring a pistol into the Lord's house, son?"

When the man didn't respond, Booe flipped open the magazine cover and turned the cylinder. The bullets dropped one by one onto the wooden floor.

He nodded to the young woman sitting beside the armed man. "Is he with you, ma'am?"

She nodded, swallowing. Booe handed her the pistol.

"If you give him back this piece or if he goes to pick up one of those cartridges before I leave the auditorium, I will gun him. Understand?"

Her voice was barely audible. "Yes."

Booe straightened and walked to the chancel, mounting the steps as the pastor backed away from the center. Booe slipped off his hat and dropped it on the communion table.

"Sorry about that, preacher. Even I know not to wear my hat in church." He glanced at the thrilled, curious face of Callie for an instant, then looked across the congregation. "I don't mean to interrupt the parson's message but momentarily, folks, and I'm not here to steal anything. I rob banks, not churches. Ain't sunk that low. I'm just here to conduct a couple items of business."

He gazed down to the wary face of George Rushing, who sat beside his wife Naomi toward the back of the room.

"Mr. George Rushing." He nodded. "When I borrowed your horse, the painted filly, three or four weeks ago, was it not the case that I promised she would be returned, unharmed." When Rushing nodded, Booe continued. "And I see this day she is here and harnessed and happy, correct?"

Again Rushing nodded.

"I hope you find this indicative of the reality that a man can be an outlaw and still be good as his word." He smiled at the farmer. "Therefore I want to offer you a deal. How much would you say the filly is worth?"

His voice was low and halting. "She's . . . not for sa—"

"But if she were and you were going to name a price for her, what would that be?"

"Uh, $200."

Booe's eyebrows arched. "Truly, George, at that price you wouldn't have to worry about selling her. Still, I want to make a trade. Tied up outside next to your wagon is a draft horse, a three-year-old trained and tried gelding named Maximus. He is accustomed to pulling timber wagons up and down mountains in the Ouachitas. You could hitch every buggy and buckboard in this county to him at once and he would have no problem pulling them straight up a hill. Maximus is of the French Percheron breed and I purchased him at a cost of $375. I offer him to you in even trade for the paint Millie."

The two men stared at one another.

"Is it a deal?"

". . . Yes."

"Thank you, Mr. Rushing. I have unharnessed Millie. Maximus being docile and not shy-of-hand, you will have no trouble hitching him to your wagon, though I expect you'll have to let out the traces."

Booe glanced at the pastor. "All but finished here, parson. I have one other thing to attend to." He looked back across the congregation. "I cannot help but notice that you all have assigned one of your young ladies, Miss Callie Dunlap, to sit up here alone on the mourner's bench." He considered his words carefully. "My assumption is that you intend for her to be called to account for some sinfulness of which you suspect her. . . . Let me tell you that I know of no other person who is as fine and worthy, as decent and upright as Miss Callie. She is, perhaps, clever and brash, prone to outsmarting those who seek to force conformation upon her, and exceedingly articulate. I am not aware, however, that any of those things are regarded in the Holy Bible as being sinful. She is, so far as I am aware, unsullied and pure. Miss Callie, therefore, is to be respected and admired more than judged and castigated. So. Shame on you Christian folks."

He gazed down from the chancel steps to where she sat, only a dozen feet away. And when he spoke, it was as if they were alone, together in the barn or on the trail. "I took a big risk coming here like this. Not the risk of coming back to Texas. Not the risk of showing myself in the daylight. I'm taking a risk with what I mean to ask you." He held out his upturned hand. "Would you come up here by me?"

She rose instantly. Her face flushed, she trembled as she stepped around the modesty rail and walked up the steps, her eyes fixed to his. He held out his left hand and took her hand and sank to a knee in the absolute silence of the moment.

"Callie Dunlap, would you grant me the great privilege of marrying me and being my wife."

For an instant she said nothing. Then, tears welling in her eyes, she spoke. "Are you going to give up robbing banks?"

He laughed. "Quick as ever, aren't you? . . . Well, I won't give up robbing banks if you won't be my wife. Cause I got no reason for quitting if you won't."

"So then, you will give up robbing banks if I marry you?"

"Yes. If you will be my wife, I will forsake robbing banks or thieving of any kind forever."

"Then yes, Richmond, I will marry you."

He felt his shoulders relax. "Good enough. You had me worried." He nodded toward the gathered worshippers. "We got a full church and a pastor. Will you do it right now?"

She nodded, tears flowing down her cheeks.

He got to his feet and looked toward the preacher, who backed up a step at his glance. Booe walked to him—the minister leaning backward as Booe approached—and took hold of his arm. He leaned close so he could whisper softly in the clergyman's ear.

"Relax, parson. There's a gold double eagle for you on the top shelf in the vestibule if you answer this next question right."

Booe backed away from him and spoke up loudly enough for the congregation to hear. "Pastor, Miss Callie and I would greatly appreciate it if you would take one more minute from the service and solemnify our vows."

The minister swallowed. "Yes. Of course." He looked out on his congregation. "Not for the sake of the blasphemers here, brethren, but in consideration of their unborn children—who have sinned not—that they receive the

106

blessing of being born in holy wedlock despite their parentage." He swallowed again. "God being the judge, it is the right of every willing soul to a Christian baptism, a Christian funeral and a Christian wedding."

Booe winked at him. He took Callie's two hands in his and faced her.

"Let me see . . . ," the pastor said, looking down. "Dearly beloved, we are gathered here in the presence of God to join together—" He glanced at the outlaw with an expression of disbelief. "—Richmond Booe and Callie Dunlap in holy matrimony. This is an honorable estate, instituted by God and signifying to us the union between Christ and his church. If any man can show just cause why these two cannot lawfully be—"

Booe cleared his throat and, when the preacher looked at him, shook his head. "Best leave that 'lawful' part out, parson. And also the 'obey' part. Obeying anybody is no more a part of this girl's nature than it is mine."

"Right." The pastor blinked and frowned, clearly trying to remember where he was in the wedding ceremony. "Uh, who gives this woman to be married to this man?"

Callie and Booe, the preacher and everyone in the church looked in the direction of George Rushing, who stared back at the couple on the chancel steps. Booe freed one hand and eased open his suit jacket, revealing the smoothly curved butt of his Colt .45.

"I do!" Rushing barked.

"Um," the preacher began, "do you, Richmond Booe, take this woman to be your wedded wife, to have and to hold, for better or worse, for richer or poorer, in sickness and in health, to love and to cherish for as long as you live, according to God's word?"

"I do."

Callie's tears burst forth. She began to sob.

"Do you, Callie Dunlap, take this man to be your wedded husband, to have and to hold, for better or worse, for richer or poorer, in sickness and in health, to love and to cherish for as long as you live, according to God's word?"

When she could not answer, low female voices from the nave encouraged her: "Go on, Callie." "Say it, Callie." "You've got to say it."

"I—do!"

The minister looked up at Booe. "I don't suppose you've got a—"

Before he could finish, Booe held open his palm. In it was a thin, gold band adorned with three green stones. He took Callie's hand and slipped the ring onto her finger.

"These emeralds are almost as pretty a green as your eyes, Callie."

She held her hand before her, turning it, her mouth open as she gazed at the ring.

"The wedding ring is the outward and visible sign of an inward and holy union, proclaiming to all the uniting of this man and woman in holy matrimony." He looked back to Booe. "Please join your right hands. . . . For inasmuch as this man and woman have consented together in holy wedlock and declared their promises to one another and demonstrated the same by vow, the receiving of a ring and the joining of their hands, I pronounce they are man and wife. What God has joined together, let not man put asunder." He leaned toward Booe and said quietly, "You may kiss the bride."

This was their second kiss and Booe was much better prepared for it. The sweet, warm tenderness of her lips was accented by the salt of her tears. He put his hand behind her head and kissed her again.

"Are you ready to go?"

"Oh yes," she replied.

Taking a deep breath, Booe faced the congregation, many of whom wore smiles. "I'm sorry for interrupting your worship, folks. We'll be on our way now." He lifted his hat off the communion table and set it back on his head. "I would ask you not to ruin Miss Callie's wedding day by forcing me to shoot any of you. You can avoid that by sitting still and listening to the rest of the parson's sermon and singing your closing hymn, just like any other Lord's day." He looked at the preacher. "I reckon you had about another thirty minutes or so to go, didn't you?"

A boy's adolescent voice called out from the back, "More like an hour."

There were a few chuckles.

"Just keep your seats for the next thirty minutes or so and we won't trouble you anymore."

He took the girl's hand and led her down the center aisle of the little sanctuary, scanning the congregation to insure their obedience. Booe opened the door just long enough for the two of them to exit the church, then shut it behind them. They stopped on the bottom step and Booe turned to look at the boy whom he had paid to watch the horses.

"Any strangers show up, pard?"

"Just you. Where you taking Miss Callie?"

"To Mexico for our honeymoon. Preacher just married us in there."

"He did not. Everybody knows he don't do weddings on Sunday."

Booe shook his head. "Boy, I can't put nothing over on you."

"Oh my Lord, Richmond." Callie was staring at the horses. "Is that Maximus?"

"He sure ain't Minimus." He followed her across the church yard as she stared at the Percheron in amazement.

"I've never seen a horse that big."

"Yeah, they use 'em up in logging country. Say, Callie, I think we ought to get a move on."

He put his arm around her waist and swung her up into the saddle on Millie's back.

"Oh." She smiled and straightened herself and took the reins in her hands as Booe handed them to her. "Thank you for trading for Millie."

Booe pulled himself onto Jack's saddle and turned toward the woods on the west side of the church. "She's your horse now, Mrs. Booe."

She caught her breath. "Oh my! I am, aren't I. I'm Mrs. Richmond Booe."

They trotted the horses to the tree line, slowing to a casual walk. Booe sighed, lifted his hat and wiped his forehead. He turned to gaze at his new wife.

"Well, you did what no lawman, bushwhacker or bounty hunter ever did. You ridded Texas of her most persistent bank robber."

She smiled at him, her face seeming to glow in the dappled sunlight.

"And you are the prettiest girl in this whole state, Callie."

"Oh." She looked down at her dress. "I'm sorry I didn't have a better outfit to wear at our wedding."

"I wouldn't worry about that. There's a fine dress shop up in Tulsa I'm taking you to. You can get a trousseau that will make the angels even more jealous. . . . I did wonder, though, why you didn't wear your new dress, the one that Constance made for you, to church."

Her smile dropped away. "Uncle said it was vain. He . . . made my aunt cut it up into an apron and rags."

Booe squirmed in his saddle. "I am sorry to hear that. Are there keepsakes you'd like to retrieve from your uncle's house before we cross the river?"

"No. Not unless we can dig up my dead dog. We do need to go there and get the money you left for me."

"Is it hid safe?"

"Oh yeah. It's well hidden."

"We'll come back for it." He nodded. "My mother's birthday is early in September. For a treat, I want to bring you down to Silman to meet her. She will be so, so proud of me. I want you to meet all my kinfolks. And when we come back across the river, we'll swing by here to pick up the last of my ill-gotten gains. It'll give me one last chance to terrorize George Rushing."

Callie laughed. She studied his face. "I was so worried about you, you know."

"You mean, after Clarksville?"

"Yes. . . . The report about the robbery came out in the Commerce newspaper. I wanted Uncle to let me read it, but he said I didn't need to think about you and those outlaws anymore, that I needed your kind out of my life once and for all. Then he went to sleep and I snuck his paper and read it."

Booe chuckled.

"I read that Jonathan died. And Mr. Bartholomew."

"Yeah. All the Kiamichi Boys were shot up except for Tom. He was sitting on the hill trying to figure out how to go down and help 'em. . . . Until I showed up. I managed to chase off the bushwhackers and get the boys back across the river. They're all on the mend at least."

"The paper said Richmond Booe was there and that he shot two men."

He looked at her. "Shot? Just shot? You mean that one feller didn't die? I'm losing my touch."

She groaned in exasperation. "I hope you were serious about giving up robbing banks, because I certainly am serious about not being married to a bank robber."

"I would never lie to you, Callie. I'm through with being an outlaw. Besides, I'm taking up being a world traveler."

She gave him a doubtful look. "Do tell."

"Yep. Got me a new bride. Prettiest flower you ever saw. I'm taking her to St. Louis and Chicago and New York City and maybe San Francisco. You know, places where they got libraries and museums and the things that can stimulate a smart mind like hers."

". . . And what are you going to do about her smart mouth?"

"Oh, I'm going to ask her lots of questions. Let her help me figure things out better than I have with all of her smart answers. Maybe we'll have a passel of smart kids."

". . . I love you, Richmond."

". . . Maybe she's not quite as smart as I thought."